A Journey

THE AUTOBIOGRAPHY OF
APOLO ANTON OHNO

❄

APOLO ANTON OHNO
WITH NANCY ANN RICHARDSON

SIMON & SCHUSTER BOOKS FOR YOUNG READERS
New York   London   Toronto   Sydney   Singapore

SIMON & SCHUSTER BOOKS FOR YOUNG READERS
An imprint of Simon & Schuster Children's Publishing Division
1230 Avenue of the Americas, New York, NY 10020
SIMON & SCHUSTER BOOKS FOR YOUNG READERS is a trademark of
Simon & Schuster.
Book design by O'Lanso Gabbidon
The text for this book is set in Garamond.
Printed in the United States of America
2 4 6 8 10 9 7 5 3 1
Library of Congress Cataloging-in-Publication Data
Ohno, Apolo Anton.
A journey: the autobiography of Apolo Anton Ohno / Apolo Anton Ohno with
Nancy Ann Richardson.
p. cm.
Summary: The autobiography of the controversial young American who won gold
and silver medals in speed skating at the 2002 Winter Olympics.
ISBN 0-689-85608-3 (hardcover)
1. Ohno, Apolo Anton—Juvenile literature. 2. Speed skaters—United States—
Biography—Juvenile literature. [1. Ohno, Apolo Anton. 2. Ice skaters. 3. Speed
skating. 4. Winter Olympic Games (19th : 2002 : Salt Lake City, Utah) 5. Japanese
Americans—Biography. 6. Youths' writings.] I. Richardson, Nancy Ann. II. Title.
GV850.O45 O45 2002
796.91'4'092—dc21
2002008766

FIRST
EDITION

This book is dedicated to all of those surrounding me. I have been truly blessed with so many loving friends and family to help me succeed in my sport. Yet I cannot leave out my fans, who have come on like a hailstorm, headlong. I especially want to thank those who see me as a person as well as an athlete. This book is for you.

Contents

Prologue

Hunger is everything. It has made me perform under the most extreme circumstances and despite the pain because above all, I want to be a champion. Hunger . . . is everything.
—Apolo Anton Ohno

The flu. That's what I caught four days before my first competition at the 2002 Salt Lake City Olympics. Fever, chills, sore throat, vomiting. My upper respiratory system was totally whacked out. I was moved from the Olympic Village, where the athletes stay for the Games, to a hotel that was closer to the Delta Center. Being a world-class athlete and becoming so sick during the biggest competition of my life messed with my mind, and at the Games, your mind needs to be totally focused.

I've always thought of myself in a sense as David versus Goliath. I have been faced with so many challenges in life and they have required me to step to a new level in order to continue the journey on my chosen path. At the 2002 Games, I lay in bed with the flu wondering why this was happening to me and trying not to panic. I had made so many mistakes since my short track career began in 1996, and so many comebacks. My road to the 2002 Games was lined with record-breaking successes and monumental failures. I went from being the youngest number-one skater in the United States, to burning out within my first year and becoming disillusioned. I faltered again, failing to make the 1998 Olympic Team and almost ended my career out of frustration at the age of fifteen. I dug deeper, and came up with nothing at first, but eventually found the inner strength to try to become number one, or better yet, to be the best I could possibly be.

I pushed my mind and body to excruciating levels of pain and made a lot of sacrifices in my quest to be a great speed skater. I also pushed away those who loved me, and only let them back into my life much later. I made another comeback, becoming the youngest skater to win the Junior World Championship. I also won the U.S. Short Track Championship and was poised to win all of my distances at the World Team Championship until I fell on the ice and slammed into the walls of the rink at thirty-five miles per hour. The impact injured my back in what would become a chronic and potentially career-ending problem.

The total failure of my immune system came next, due to the pressures of being a fifteen-year-old kid managing my own equipment, traveling around the globe, intensely training and not paying attention to my body. I slid down the mountain I'd fought so hard to climb, slipping constantly and struggling. But my inability to understand my body's needs and the physical and emotional tolls of my sport resulted in a complete burnout. I had to push through recurrent illnesses that stole confidence, strength, and power; U.S. Speedskating federation politics; changing coaches; improper weight and training programs; loneliness; fears; frustrations. Not always gracefully, I leaped over each hurdle, sometimes banging my knees so hard that the blows will never be forgotten.

The 2000-2001 season was my true breakout season. By its end I'd claimed twelve victories on the World Cup circuit—four in the 1500-meter, one in the 1000-, three in the 500-, and four in the 3000-meter. I was dominating like no other skater. But early in 2001 a second and much more serious back injury threatened to take me away from my sport. With only seven months before the 2002 Olympic Trials, I needed three months of intensive rehabilitation to be able to perform at 80 percent of my abilities. I couldn't skate or train and I saw my Olympic dreams sliding away along with my fitness with each day, week, and month. The mental toll of knowing that my predicted performance level after rehabilitation would still only be 80 percent was brutal.

I refused to give up. Four months before the Games I started to train hard again. Agonizing muscle spasms ripped through my back and forced me off the ice at first, but with each day I improved. When I made it to the Olympic Trials, I was thrilled by how far I had come. When I qualified to skate in each individual event in the Games, plus the relay, I felt like I'd reached the top of the mountain. I had given 110 percent to get there and was euphoric.

So why is this happening to me? I wondered as I lay in bed with the flu four days before my first Salt Lake City Olympic event, the 1000-meter preliminaries. My mind raced . . . I was healthy the day before. My back was feeling better. I was finally at the Olympics after years of fighting illnesses and injuries. Why is this happening? This is the Olympics and athletes are showing everything they've got. With only three months of extremely weak training I'd made it to the Games, but I was sick when I was supposed to be at my best.

The doctors offered to give me antibiotics. They were necessary at that point, but they're never a cure for me. My body isn't used to drugs, so I react strongly to antibiotics. They make me tired and slow, and basically I can't even get out of bed the next day. Four days before Wednesday's preliminary trials, where I would have to place well in order to get into the Saturday 1000-meter Olympic finals, all I wanted to do was sleep, and I had trouble walking to the bathroom without sniffling, watering eyes, and dizziness. Apolo Anton Ohno, the supposed big threat in short track skating, was being brought to his knees by wracking coughs, fever, and a shot of antibiotics in his ass.

My father stepped in to help me with my program of hydration and detoxification, but I improved slowly, not in leaps and bounds. Still, by the time of the prelims I was on the upswing. I forgot about the flu the moment I walked into the packed arena.

The noise was deafening. Tens of thousands of fans had come to watch short track, and because of NBC's coverage they knew my name and chanted it over and over again. There was a sea of supportive signs that I wish I'd had time to read. I felt a tremendous surge of energy, but tried to keep my cool. When I stepped onto the ice, I had trouble hearing myself think, and the cheering made my ears buzz and my teeth chatter. There was no time to consider the last few days. It simply was not a question anymore of whether I was ready—I was going to skate, and I was there to compete well. I put my head down and did what I had to do, qualifying through my preliminaries and heats. By the time I returned to the hotel, I was slated to race on Saturday.

I have never experienced a race like the 1000-meter final. Though many people look at it and say, "Well, that's short track," it's not true. I have never witnessed or been involved in a race like that one; never. This time I was ready for the electricity of the crowd and after a moment of appreciation, I used the cheers as energy and tuned out the noise. The lineup was fierce—China's Jiajun Li, Canada's Mathieu Turcotte, South Korea's Hyun-Soo Ahn, and Australia's Steven Bradbury. I got off the line well, reserving my strength and drafting off the front skaters until I was ready to make my move. With four laps to go I was in perfect position and started to surge. At two laps I pulled into the lead in front of Ahn. The fans went into a frenzy and their energy was like a bolt of electricity. I pushed harder and was seconds away from winning the race.

On the final turn Li attempted an outside pass, tangling arms with me and slowing my speed. He fell, slid into the pads, and eventually was disqualified. Since I'd slowed, Ahn tried to pass on the inside, even though there was no room. He fell too, and his right hand grabbed at my left leg in a last-ditch effort to stay on his feet. The grab sent me into a spin and I landed on my backside before crashing into the wall.

Sometimes, if I'm about to pull off a crazy move as I'm going down, a fall will occur in slow motion. There was no slow motion during this fall. I went down fast and hit hard. My head slammed into the pads and then ricocheted off. During the fall I caught my left inner thigh with my own blade and gashed my leg, but didn't even notice it at the time. Turcotte had also been taken out by Ahn and lay on the ice beside me. Steven Bradbury of Australia, who'd been in the back, well over ten meters behind the pack, skated across the finish line and won as the "last man standing."

I don't know what possessed me to scramble to my feet, to fall yet again and then rise, my leg numb from the wound and slick with blood that pooled to the edge of my skate and puddled inside. Maybe it was instinct . . . I don't know . . .

Tussling Whales

I done something new for this fight. I done wrassled with an alligator. That's right, I done wrassled an alligator, tussled with a whale, handcuffed lightning and threw thunder in jail. Last week I murdered a rock, hospitalized a brick. I'm so mean I make medicine sick.

—Muhammad Ali

Muhammad Ali is my man, the greatest boxer and perhaps athlete of all time. As a kid, I used to go to the bookstore and read all about him. Every book report I ever did was on him. He was the best. He'd say, "I'm gonna knock him out in three," and then he'd knock out his opponent in three rounds. You don't get better than that in a sport. Predicting to beat your opponent, that's normal, but to know the exact moment is incredible.

"If Ali says a mosquito can pull a plow, don't ask how. Hitch him up!" Ali revolutionized boxing and showed that heavyweights could also be fast. He won a gold medal at the 1960 Olympics and was the three-time Heavyweight Champion of the World. I respect his abilities, and also his spirit.

Today Muhammad Ali has found a different arena to fight in. He has Parkinson's disease and is working to find a cure. That makes him even more of a legend in my eyes.

❊ ❊ ❊

> Pain is temporary. It may last a minute, or an hour, or a day, or a year, but eventually it will subside and something else will take its place. If I quit, however, it lasts forever.
>
> —Lance Armstrong

Lance Armstrong is another one of my heroes. Just like Ali, he's faced the worst and keeps fighting. He's beaten testicular cancer that had spread to his lungs and brain, a miraculous feat on its own, and gone on repeatedly to win the Tour de France, the most grueling bike race in the world.

"I don't always win," Armstrong said. "Sometimes just finishing is the best I can do. But with each race, I feel that I further define my capacity for living." He's an amazing individual with the cardiovascular system of ten horses, and he's a true, pure athlete who came back from death to rise above the clouds.

❊ ❊ ❊

> He is a man with nothing in his personal life to distract him, nothing in his emotional makeup to undermine him; in short there is nothing controllable that he will fail to control. He is an arrow shaved of all superfluity, feathered strictly for aerodynamics, drawn and discharged with the barest expenditure of motion, an arrow streaming nowhere except to its target.
>
> —Gary Smith, *Sports Illustrated*

Michael Johnson is an Olympic runner who won two gold medals at the 1996 Atlanta Games and is considered by many to be the greatest sprinter of all time. I've always admired his unorthodox style and the way his pure concentration consistently showed the world his determination. Unlike other runners, Johnson broke the stereotype that if you ran the 200-meter, you also ran the 100-, but if you ran the 400-, that's all you did. Johnson did it all, and changed the rules of the sport in the process.

At the Atlanta Games, wearing customized gold-colored track shoes, Johnson ran both the 200- and 400-meter—an unprecedented performance. He set an Olympic record in the 400 and won the 200 also in record time, the latter at a speed experts thought was humanly possible but believed would be achieved by some unborn athlete of the future. "I'd like to be remembered as nothing more than what I am, the most consistent and versatile sprinter who ever sprinted," Johnson told reporters after the Games. "No one has ever done what I've done over a period of time at the distances I've run. There can be no doubters left now."

The thing is, about 80 percent of the time people who are born with talent don't use it to their full potential. And the people who work the hardest, most of the time don't have the natural talent. Ali, Armstrong, and Johnson have the talent and work the hardest. It's a powerful combination.

The idea that I might inspire anyone the way Ali, Armstrong, and Johnson have inspired me is surreal. My nickname was Chunkie when I was a kid, and all of my friends had nicknames like Worm, Checkered, Little T, Alpha, Sleepy, and Cupid. I grew up in a single-parent household and was lucky enough to have a father who recognized my potential as an athlete at a young age. I've seen gangs and fights but I never really lived in that world. And though I've overcome the obstacles put in my way, I have yet to "handcuff lightning and throw thunder in jail," although I like to think that I could.

I look around at other athletes and still want to learn from them. I love watching basketball, especially Michael Jordan. Those guys are sick athletes—explosive and almost as fast as Superman. In April of 2002 I had the chance to talk with LaVar Arrington, linebacker for the

Washington Redskins. Being a curious athlete, I tried to pick LaVar's brain. He told me that he does a series of routine preparations before each game, but the one that caught my attention was that he always listens to the craziest, sickest music possible. When he goes out on the field, he's an animal running through walls. Jeff Garcia, quarterback for the San Francisco 49ers, says that when big guys come at him he doesn't even think about getting hurt. He's in the zone—totally untouchable. I like to hear how different athletes work, and what techniques help them perform. It makes me better, but does it make me more of an inspiration?

I guess what I want people to take away from watching me compete, if anything, is that I come back stronger than anybody else. When I lose, I get down on myself and never blame the condition of the ice or other skaters. I always blame things that were in my control, even though about half of short track isn't actually controllable. Though I'm too tough on myself sometimes, I really learn from my mistakes. I love to compete—every minute of it, from the disappointments to the successes.

I'm still learning. And I imagine my heroes are in the background, watching me and waiting for greatness. There are moments, like the 2002 Olympics or the way I carried myself in the midst of controversies that threatened my mental and physical abilities, when I hope I'm making them proud. But I'm still the same guy who likes to steal my roommate Shani Davis's food just to make him mad. I'll make sure to eat half of something and then leave the other half and the wrapper out just to mess with him.

As I write this book, I have to answer the question of whether or not I'm a hero for kids in the way Lance, Michael, and Ali are to me. It's a powerful question and I guess the answer is that for some athletes and kids I am. Whatever positive things anyone can take from my life, they're welcome to them. I just hope that in the future I'll have the chance to give even more.

My life has not been daisies, and I want kids to understand I've struggled and overcome difficulties. Maybe someday a kid will go to the bookstore and spend hours reading about me the way I did about Ali. The idea is both slightly uncomfortable and exciting to me because there are so many chapters left to write in my life and I hope it's a very long (and impressive) story. I honestly don't know what battles I'm going to face next, only that I have the spirit and the will to face anything and fight for my sport and for what I believe is right. I'll give 110 percent and still dig down deeper for more.

My father is the man who taught me to always give 110 percent. To understand who I am, you have to understand who he is and where he came from. He's one of my heroes too, and my partner in short track. I'm a kid who used to never like being told what to do by anyone, but my dad has been my mentor and guide. He is a very wise man and seems to know something about everything. He has educated and protected me for nineteen years, and sometimes I know it's hard seeing me grown up. I think he's afraid of losing our relationship and partnership, but I'll always want and need him in my life.

My dad was born in Tokyo, Japan. His father was a state university vice president. From kindergarten on, he was on the educational fast track there, which is like aiming for an Ivy League school, but more competitive because there are fewer colleges to choose from. In Japan parents push their kids so hard in school because it promises job security and safety.

Dad's early life was spent studying and every year he had to take tests in order to achieve the next level in school. It's not like the U.S., where you hear of kids getting passed to the next grade before they can read or write. If you don't pass the tests in Japan, you don't move on and that puts you on a different, less prestigious and lower-income career path. Pretty much, one mess-up and it's over.

In high school Dad slept five hours a night and spent his waking hours cramming, memorizing, and practicing for exams. He did what his parents expected of him and never questioned the hard work or his own desires. He progressed every year, but there was never time to enjoy his success because each year involved another enormous test. One day in high school he looked around his classroom and noticed that everyone's expression was the same—just a mask of concentration, because they were all working toward a university education and there was a lot of pressure. My dad decided he didn't want to be there anymore.

At age eighteen, and speaking only rudimentary English, my father came to the United States. He'd wanted to visit for some time, but had no idea that he was going to stay. He ended up in Portland, Oregon. His parents were very disappointed when he didn't come home, but Dad was young, happy, and had very few responsibilities. He worked as a janitor, waiter, newspaper deliveryman, bartender, you name it, and then decided he wanted to travel to Seattle. The problem was, he pronounced it "Sheetle," and nobody understood when he asked for directions. He always jokes that one of the greatest things about Americans is their willingness to try to figure out what a foreigner is saying. In Europe, if they don't understand you, they slam the door. Eventually Dad found his way to Seattle.

Somehow, between looking for new jobs, my dad ended up in beauty school. He won a contest within the first year. He'd spent so long struggling to figure out what he wanted to do with his life, and it suddenly became clear. My father has an artistic personality and he'd found his outlet. In the early seventies Dad traveled to London, which at the time was packed with artists. Hairdressing there was a higher skill, and he studied at the Vidal Sassoon school at the height of its popularity. There he learned the precision cut—haircutting that doesn't depend upon curlers or dryers but upon the cut itself to make the shape. At the time it was a revolutionary idea. He had tons of friends, visited salons to watch stylists work, and studied haircutting like it was sculpture. The lifestyle was nonstop, and my dad had a blast.

By the time he returned to Seattle, my father was in demand and did a lot of teaching and training in addition to his own work as a stylist. He was a workaholic, applying in his new profession his ability to study long hours. The powerful difference now was that he loved his job and was driven to succeed.

Back then if you had three thousand dollars in your pocket you could open your own salon. With a partner he opened his first shop. It had a rubber tree growing inside, and the branches covered the walls and ceiling. He says it felt like a jungle and the landlord hung an enormous marine chain from the wall and trickling water ran down the metal rings so that it sounded like the rainforest. Dad cut two-handed and moved quickly from client to client. They didn't mind because he was so good. When he wasn't cutting, he traveled back to Europe to learn more.

In the early 1980s my dad met my mother. They married and I was born in 1982. The media has reported that my mother left us when I was a year old. That's true. My dad has been a single father for nineteen years. It's also been written that I don't know my mother. That's true too. My father and I never talk about her because I have no interest in knowing her. It doesn't upset me and I'm not angry. I simply don't miss her, because she isn't in my memory and it's hard to miss something you've never had.

Some of the media is intent on exploring my relationship with my mother. I tell them there's nothing to explore because I honestly know as much about her as they do. My father and his family are my family. My friends and loved ones are my family. Maybe I would have turned out softer or less stubborn if I'd had a mom and been showered with affection. Then again, maybe I wouldn't have had the warrior instinct or the hunger to succeed. I never think of my mother. She was a biological donor and I'm grateful that she carried me inside her for nine months. But she was never my mom.

My dad's life changed when he became a single father. He used to wear fancy suits and shiny shoes to work, but after he took over the full responsibility for me, he didn't have the time to dress up or polish his shoes. He lost a lot of friends because he no longer went to late-night parties but spent his evenings at home. Some of his friends felt sorry for him, but he changed his life willingly.

Dad had no relatives nearby to help him out, and depended on good day care. He'd drop me off in the morning, work until 7 or 8 P.M. and then pick me up. There was no choice—he was the sole provider. He remembers being one of the only men to take his kid into the day care center, and that at first he felt inadequate because all the moms brought special blankets and stuffed animals for their kids and he hadn't thought of that. He was also confused by all the different types of bottles he saw—he'd thought there was only one kind. Dad learned to take care of me the same way I first learned sports, by watching and copying people who seemed to know what they were doing.

There's a story my father always tells. He bought me a small bicycle and training wheels when I was only five. He took the bike out of the trunk of his car and put it on the sidewalk, then turned around to get the training wheels. When he looked up, I'd already gotten on the bike and taken off. My first time on a two-wheeler and I wobbled a bit, but didn't fall. I learned from watching other people. My dad did the same with raising a child. He asked a lot of questions, listened carefully, and pushed through the confusion (and, at times, fear).

I remember the first hill I ever rode down on that bike. In the beginning my eyes were wide with fear, but as I took off I felt the exhilaration of being in control and the speed of flying. I remember the flash of green trees from the corner of my vision and hearing my dad laughing.

There were difficult times. Finding dependable day care, especially on Saturdays, was really tough for Dad, but sometimes he had clients on the weekends and he couldn't turn down the opportunity to make money to support us. He spent a lot of time checking out so-called licensed providers and was frightened to discover little kids belted to their car seats in front of the television—crying or dirty or just zoned out. In other places the "day care professionals" were encouraging kids to punch each other or hadn't thought to clean their establishment, resulting in filthy conditions. My dad spent a lot of time researching day care and was very careful and wary before he'd let anyone take care of me.

Dad spent every possible weekend with me. He'd plan special trips to the mountains or ocean so that we'd have time to bond and he could pass on his love of the outdoors. He liked to take me on adventures, and he'd pull off the highway onto narrow logging trails so that we could discover new places—deserted mountain lakes mirroring the forests and peaks. There were warm light rains that made everything smell more alive, and the sweet scent of wild strawberries on our skin. At night we gazed at the stars and he'd tell me stories about the constellations that weren't always right but were still a lot of fun.

We did some camping and spent holidays and summer vacations at Iron Springs Resort, which is on the Washington coast near a town named Copalis. Iron Springs has simple wood cottages, each with a kitchen, living room, and bedroom, and porches that overlook the

Pacific. You open your front door, and all you see is the gray sand and dark green water. On each side of the resort, water runs down in mountain streams so that you are isolated from the public and have an entire beach to yourself. No cars can drive by and tourists rarely visit. We'd watch the seagulls taking their morning bath, walk along the sand and climb to the tops of dunes—I'd jump down over and over again, plummeting into soft piles of sand. It made me feel like I could fly. When we returned to the cottage, we'd draw pictures of what we'd seen and learned.

During one of those early trips, my dad explained my name to me. He found it in a dictionary right after I was born. "Ap" means to steer away from and "lo" means look out, here he comes. He liked the meaning and the message and that's why he named me Apolo.

With my dad, our weekend trips weren't just about the adventures. He believed that the time we spent driving in the car was important too. You can really get to know your kid by spending hours and hours on a long drive. A half hour in the morning, after school, or during a rushed dinner isn't enough time to have a deep conversation with a nine-year-old. But six or ten hours in a car, with no outside influences, no television or phone or friends stopping by, allowed my dad to understand me better and hear details about my life, friends, and sports. He'd always initiate the conversations, and later I grew to understand that after a hectic week of work, it was his way of gauging school, happiness, friendships, and my needs.

From the start, Dad tried to be everything his father was not. He has a great relationship with his dad and he loves him, but Grandfather was typical of his generation and didn't really communicate. My dad tells the story of going to a baseball game in Tokyo with his dad. He was about five years old and didn't know anything about the sport. They sat in the stands and his father was silent throughout the game. Dad didn't understand what was happening—the rules, the scoring system, why batters struck out and had to leave the field without running the bases. His father never explained the game to him, not before or after. He spent the night wondering about baseball and how it really worked.

A father is supposed to teach his child everything he can—break it down so it's easier to understand, offer advice, even if his child doesn't ask for it or know he needs it. My dad has always tried to explain things, and then to apply what I've learned to a larger life picture to give me perspective. It requires patience and time, but it's part of being a dad.

My dad doesn't care about being rich or famous at all. He's lived in the same townhouse my whole life. When he comes home late at night it's always freezing, because he turns the heat off during the day to save money. There's no food in the fridge since I left home—maybe soy sauce, butter, soy milk, and orange juice, but nothing you could really put together to make a meal. Dad usually eats out because he's a crazy hard worker who puts in long days and late nights, at his salon and in everything he handles for my skating. He cares about the quality of his life and mine, but he measures that in our mutual connection and successes, not in things.

By the time I was three years old, Dad says he realized that I was gifted in many ways. I was a quick reader, musical, and extremely agile. Most of all, I picked things up very quickly. My dad felt he had a responsibility to help me live up to my potential and, as long as I could take it, push me to a higher level. When my first teacher called him in for a conference and said I was not paying attention in class (I'd walked away during a French lesson, picked a book from the shelf, and started to read), my dad figured out that I was bored and found a better school.

My dad didn't focus just on school, because he wanted to give me the balance in life he hadn't had as a kid. When I was six, he enrolled me in swimming. I started out in a small district program with kids of every level who had to proceed through six stages before they were allowed to race on the team. Dad watched me practice, saw that I was goofing around and wasn't being challenged, and found a private swim club. The private swim coach was willing to check out my abilities, so Dad took me over one afternoon. I remember watching the other kids swim like fish. They had amazing technique and I just got in the water and splashed around as hard and as fast as I could. Surprisingly I kept up and the coach said I could stay. I learned all the strokes quickly and began to compete. I was only going to practice three days a week and most of the other children went six, but I wanted to win.

My father dreamed that I would attend Stanford University. He'd watched Stanford cream the University of Washington at a meet and believed that everything they did to win was "scientific." I just remember that Stanford had two plush massage tables next to the swimming pool. Before swimmers would jump into the water and after they finished their event they'd get a rubdown. The University of Washington swimmers just looked cold and miserable.

But I wasn't involved just in swimming. Before puberty I had a three-octave voice and my father enrolled me in the Northwest Boys' Choir. I hated it but now understand he was only trying to keep me busy. In addition I started roller-skating at the local rink, which was social, fun, and great to do when you grow up in the Pacific Northwest and it's always raining.

One day when I was very young my dad was at work and I made a fire in the hearth with two kids from across the street. We put every piece of paper we could find into the flames. Of course, we hadn't known to open the flue and by the time my father got home the living room was filled with a gray haze and there were ashes flying everywhere. The entire house smelled of smoke. But I didn't get spanked for getting our home dirty. The fire had threatened my safety and scared my father.

Dad always encouraged me to have friends. When I was a little older, between all my activities, I found time to hang out and go to as many parties as I could. But I was always the first one to be picked up. Some of my friends could stay out as late as 2 or 3 A.M. but my dad would pick me up at 11:30 because I had meets on the weekends, and also because, though he wanted me to be social, he believed trouble happens after midnight.

"If you're an alcoholic or have an addictive personality you won't find out until after you start drinking and doing drugs, and then it will be too late." That's what my dad had to say about partying. It was never an issue for me because I have always had mad energy and I don't need to have more. I like to experience everything clearly so that I'm always in control and I'm very happy to enjoy things straight-up.

That's not to say that Dad and I didn't clash, especially once I hit puberty. We fought about school because I'd blown off the honor program. We fought about weekends, because if I didn't have a meet then I'd make plans to go to parties instead of on road trips with him. Typical father-son stuff—I was pushing him away, attempting independence, and he was pulling me back, trying to guide and protect me. The thing is, my dad had to face it all as a single parent. He couldn't play good cop-bad cop with a wife or girlfriend. If he was too extreme, he'd alienate me. If he was too soft, I'd alienate him. Around that time my dad started having a tough time keeping me on track. We had different plans.

The good news for me was that once I hit puberty, my voice changed and I could no longer hit the high notes. Thank God and good-bye Northwest Boys' Choir. I started to hang out with this kid during my free time. His family was wealthy and lived in a big home, and it seemed like his parents pretty much let him do whatever he wanted. I loved it at his house. Dad never wanted me to spend the night there, but I did countless times. He'd raised me in a more conservative, disciplined lifestyle where every spare moment was used effectively and I started kickin' it at my friend's house and getting comfortable *not* always moving forward to the next thing.

My dad was pretty frustrated with me. He felt like everyone was against him, including the hormones coursing through my body as a result of puberty. But he had a schedule and no matter what he had to do, he was going to make me stick to it. He'd seen many parents who let their kids make life choices even though they had no understanding of life at that age. When it came to big decisions, my dad refused to give in. He didn't want me to look back on missed opportunities with regret and ask, "Why didn't you stop me? Why'd you let me get away with this or that?" He firmly believed that if he let his child decide his own life path, it would lead to disaster.

I started to hang out with older kids—sixteen, seventeen, eighteen—when I was only thirteen. For some reason I just related better to them, and usually they thought I was their age. One day my dad came home when I was supposed to be at swim practice. Instead I was hanging out with these two older guys. My dad told them they'd better get going. They replied that they didn't have a ride.

"Well, how did you get here in the first place?" Dad asked. "I'm not going to give you a ride, and don't come back here anymore because Apolo has a lot of things to do." He literally threw them out.

In hindsight my dad may have been right about a few of my friends. Some are now in college, others have good jobs, but a couple are still doing the same things they were doing as kids, which is okay, but at the same time kind of sad. I love my friends, all of them, no matter what. But I know that I was lucky. I had heroes, dreams of wrestling alligators, and was blessed with athletic gifts.

Just for Fun

My favorite book as a child was *Green Eggs and Ham* by Dr. Seuss. I liked the idea of the stubborn critter in a tall droopy black hat refusing to eat those nasty green eggs and ham. He just couldn't be tricked or bribed—and he wouldn't eat them on a train, or in a house, or with a mouse. In my imagination I was that stubborn critter—wily and too smart to try green food. When I was a kid, I wouldn't do *anything* I didn't want to do . . . unless my dad insisted. And still, I found ways around him.

My entire skating career started for fun. When I was seven years old, my father would take me to the roller-skating rink every Thursday after school. It was an enormous rink crowded with tons of kids and video games, which I didn't get into until much later. There were kids who went to the rink just to play the games and never even skated. But I'd get out there on my quad skates (two wheels in the front, two in the back) and skate as fast as I could. I loved speed and right away I wanted to race. My father was game.

My first quad race was in Lynwood, Washington, and I got second place. Man, I hated it! My dad was proud and the trophy was pretty tight—a little pop can that I thought was cool. But I hadn't won and I was a little kid and upset. Defeat has never come easily to me. Meanwhile, other kids in the sport were practicing six days a week. I'd just go to the rink, skate as fast as I could for a few hours, goof around with my buddies, and then go home. Both my father and I looked upon roller-skating as recreational.

I continued to swim, and by the time I was twelve, I'd won the state championship in breaststroke. My father still had visions of Stanford, but I was starting to hate swim practice—the redundancy of laps, cold water, and long hours of muscle-numbing freestyle, backstroke, butterfly, and breaststroke. I liked skating more than the pool. I joined a local rink in Auburn, Washington. John Guftason, the owner, was a laid-back guy who didn't really coach but cared about each kid.

When I first saw in-line skates (four wheels in a straight line) I had to get a pair. My dad, who saw how fast I already was, and how much I loved skating, agreed. At my first race, I was the only kid using in-line skates. I beat everyone easily because you glide more on in-lines and they're just faster. I felt like I'd cheated. After that race all those other kids started using in-lines. For the next two years my father drove me to every race we could possibly attend. He had a little brown Volkswagen Rabbit. It looked like it had no paint on it and had rusted into its brownish color.

My dad had crazy endurance and he used to drive all night, even through blinding snowstorms, to get me to a race when I was too young to drive. I remember waking up in the middle of a storm on our way to Springfield, Missouri, and my dad's hair and face were soaking wet. When I asked why, he said not to worry, he had been trying to get us out of a ditch. He had skidded off the road, and after attempting to push us out, he'd decided to rock the tiny car back and forth until he had enough momentum to get over the snowbank. He did, but then the highway out of Denver was closed.

We traveled winding back roads in a car without four-wheel drive through snow that fell so hard you couldn't see a foot in front of the windshield, and we made it to Missouri at 2 A.M. Dad had gotten us to the race on time by driving twenty hours straight. Crazy-crazy-crazy!

Sometimes my dad would go to work at the salon all day, then get in the car and drive through the night while I slept in the back. There were close calls—a competition in Michigan where my dad forgot the time change and the judges were scratching my name off the roster as we ran into the arena. We weren't rich so there weren't many plane flights, but we made it work because my dad believed it was his job to get me to competitions.

My days were filled with morning practices in the pool, school, and then skating in the afternoon. When the media writes that I spent my childhood as a latchkey kid, I just have to laugh. Yes, my dad worked long hours at his salon and I made my own dinners from food he bought and organized for me (lasagna, spaghetti, chicken, and burgers), but I wasn't sitting at home watching TV and eating chips. I had an insane amount of energy as a kid, and when I wasn't swimming or skating, I was riding my bike, playing football with friends, or outside just messing around.

My thirteenth year ended with a large local club competition. The grand finale was a 3000-meter race with all age groups skating together. I'd skated against the senior guys and always did well, but I didn't think I had a chance to place. Still, it meant a lot to me to do well. I remember skating as hard as I could, rounding a corner and suddenly feeling a huge push from behind. One of the seniors, KC, who is now a long tracker, had given me a push so that I could go faster.

KC was much older and could have easily beaten me, but he saw how hard I was trying and wanted to help. He was a cool cat then and he still is today. I came in second and I was super happy. KC probably doesn't even remember the race—he was doing long track by then and his in-line skating was pretty much over. It's strange how a single, important moment in one person's life might not even be memorable to another.

The magical year my dad and I watched short track skating for the first time was 1994. It was the Albertville Olympics and all I remember is thinking about how fast (up to thirty-five miles per hour) the skaters circled the rink. My dad was captivated too.

Short track originated in Europe more than a hundred years ago. By 1906 skaters in the United States began to take part in competitions and by the 1920s crowds would fill Madison Square Garden in Manhattan to watch the U.S. and Canada short track skaters race. They saw what I saw in 1994—speed, sharp blades, tight corners, and the threat of contact and falls. After World War II, Europeans and the Far East began to catch on to the sport. It was a demonstration event in the 1988 Olympics and in 1994 became a full Olympic sport.

Today there are four official short track Olympic events. The 500-meters is a sprint, the 1000-meters is a midlength race, the 1500-meters is an endurance race, and the 5000-meter relay is a team race. In the 5000- each team is made of four members who can trade off at any time, in any order, by touch or push. Changeovers usually happen when successors pick up speed in the inner zone and then move onto the track at the perfect moment to get a push from behind. Only one skater can skate the final two laps. It's a brutally long race, the ice gets chewed up, and by the last few laps it's hard to hold an edge in the turns. Another event, which is not part of the Olympics but demands similar endurance to the 5000-meters, is the individual 3000-meters that is raced at the national and international competitions.

Short track skaters skate indoors on a 111-meter track. There are four to six skaters in each event and we race against each other, not the clock. Nine- and four-lap time trials are used in national competitions to cull the top sixteen skaters from the rest of the pack, and also as part of a point system that gets added to individual tallies given for finishing each race. Time is used only to mark speed records. Measured to the inches, there are seven rubber cones called "blocks," set up on each side of the course and they mark the turns. When the starting signal goes off, skaters sprint for the first turn and establish their positions. If you're in front you don't have to use energy to pass other skaters, but there's no one to draft off (skate behind to decrease wind resistance) so it's more tiring.

Speed skating isn't just about endurance and who can go faster. There's a lot of technique in holding your blade through a turn; deciding when to pass another skater; or choosing to stay in the back, draft, and wait for a gap or chance to pass. Skaters can also be disqualified for charging off the starting line, inside impeding (passing on the left) and outside impeding (causing interference while passing on the right). Additionally, the referees can DQ a skater for cross-tracking, which means cutting in front of another skater and impeding their progress. It's unusual to fall and still win a race because the turns are sharp, the track is small, and once you hit the padded walls of the rink you're usually out of the game.

Refereeing short track skating is a tough job. Things happen so fast and sometimes rulings appear more subjective than factual. Skaters *know* when they've done something wrong, but anything can happen in short track and usually does. And since there are preliminary rounds, quarterfinals, semifinals, and finals in most major competitions, it's tough to count on smooth races without problems. People got the chance to see it at the Olympics. It's what makes the sport of short track so tough and fulfilling.

It's hard to believe I had the time to pick up a new sport, but after the 1994 Olympics I just had to learn how to do short track. "Santa" brought me a pair of speed skates for Christmas, but I didn't know how to use them. My dad asked around and found out that there was a short track club in Eugene, Oregon. We drove down five hours to

Eugene for my first race. I had never been on skates or the ice before that day.

This is another example of the kindness of others not being forgotten. When I stepped onto the ice, I really thought I could easily make the switch from in-line skates to short track. I soon found that my biggest problem was gliding. All of the other skaters were effortlessly circling the rink and I wasn't going anywhere. I was pushing and sweating and my dad was looking down from the stands with a puzzled expression on his face. He thought that maybe I just needed to keep circling to break in the blades.

Finally another skater stopped beside me. "You have to sharpen your skates," he said.

"What do you mean?"

"When they're new, the edges are serrated. You sharpen them until the ridges are gone so you can glide."

"Oh . . . right."

I didn't know anything about my equipment. Skate blades (from twelve to eighteen inches in length depending on your height, body weight, foot size, and technical ability) are made from a bimetal, which isn't two metals, but one that has two different hardnesses. Then there's the bend. The bend for a blade is unique for each athlete. It's usually a smooth arc that follows the directional bend in the corner of the skating track. Bends can increase stability and help with tight turns, but they're less efficient in the straightaways.

The rocker is the most technical aspect of blades and is usually the reason a skater feels "off" at practice or a competition. The rocker is the curvature of the bottom of the blade, and it's usually a constant radius with the high point at the middle of the blade. Every time you sharpen your skates, you can slightly alter the rocker. A skater has to know what feels right, what feels wrong, and eventually learn how to fix it himself or find a great mechanical coach who is extremely talented at making almost imperceptible changes to the blades. Usually it's a combination of a skater *and* their coach because it's so difficult to make a skate perfect.

I didn't know any of these things during my first short track race in Eugene. I also had never heard of the concept of the offset. A blade is offset on a boot, meaning the blade is moved slightly to the left to allow skaters to lean farther in their turns without the left side of their boot contacting the ice, which can result in a fall. Offsetting is a way to counter the strong centrifugal force that acts on skaters in tight turns by using their bodies' lean. Every athlete uses a different amount of offset, which can increase speed and performance if it feels good.

After I sharpened my blades during the Eugene competition, I thought they were perfect. But there was a little girl who still beat me three times. Blond hair, a ponytail, a satisfied grin. I was so pissed off and tired and she made it look so easy. I started to copy her style and beat her the last race. I never fell that first day, but I left the rink thinking that short track was freezing compared to the warm rinks of in-line, and that I had a lot to learn.

Dad and I started to drive up to Vancouver, British Columbia, on the weekends because short track is much bigger in Canada. There were competitions held at a local rink during the winter, it was a shorter drive than to Eugene, and there were strong skaters up there to learn from and watch. I didn't have a coach, so those weekends were practice, training, and competition for me. Dad had been taping swim meets for years, so he brought his camera up to BC and taped each event. During the weeks I'd watch the tapes and try to learn from my mistakes and others' successes.

What I remember most was how smooth skating began to feel. Smooth and quiet. There was another nice change too. None of the skaters in BC talked "trash." Everyone talks trash at in-line competitions . . . everyone. "You gonna give me this race, right? You're not going to take this race from me, 'cause you know you're tired from the last race." They think they're so good and it's hilarious and I loved it. I was right in there, talking smack and trying to intimidate with the best. But in short track no one talks like that . . . no one. When I first made the switch the other skaters looked at me like I was insane and I learned pretty quickly to keep quiet.

I also learned how to improve, got faster, and started to really compete, but still didn't know much about technique or taking care of my own equipment. In January 1996 I came out of nowhere at the U.S. Junior World Championship Trials and placed fourth overall. I actually could have skated even better, but during the 1000-meter race I was in third and made a bad pass, bumping one of the top guys. I felt so badly about it because I was a "nobody" who wasn't going to make the team so I told myself to go back to the pack (my own punishment) and I just hung there until the end of the race.

I was crazy nervous during that junior trials competition. In hindsight there wasn't much pressure. I was just a fourteen-year-old kid and there were no expectations of me going in. There was no bull's-eye on my back like there is today, and it's always easier not to be targeted. There were no young guys shooting for me and looking at my weaknesses as if I was in a fishbowl being followed by piranhas.

I really respect guys like Marc Gagnon, a Canadian skater out of Montreal who's been on top for almost ten years, is a four-time World Overall Champion, and won a gold in the 1998 Olympics as part of the men's relay team. During his six peak-performance years he never came in less than second place. He is consistently the guy to beat, but he's maintained his edge even though everyone is looking to dust him. It's harder to be on top than to be the underdog—any competitor can tell you that. It's harder and lonelier to be on top, and the pressure can be exhausting.

I miss the old days sometimes, when I'd go to a competition and make a friend like Shani Davis. Shani's from Chicago and he was the 1500-meter Junior World Champion, and the first American to make two junior world teams (short and long track) in one year. More recently he was first overall at the 2000 U.S. Junior Short Track Championships; first overall at the 2001 U.S. Junior Long Track Championships; and a qualifier for the 2002 Olympic Team.

Until Shani, I didn't have many friends on the short track circuit. They both feared me because I had a background as an in-liner that gave me great endurance, and disliked me because I'd come over from in-line and a lot of short trackers look down on that sport. Neither Shani nor I were good enough at the time to care about any of that. We were young and we wanted to have fun, eat tons of candy before races, and listen to rap music.

Of course, you know what happens at the end of *Green Eggs and Ham,* right? Sam finally convinces the critter in the tall black hat to try the food. Exasperated, he does . . . and discovers he actually likes green eggs and ham. Unfortunately, life doesn't always mirror children's books. At the end of 1996 a single phone call changed my fate. As a result, I was forced to give in to my father's wishes, which led to unforgettable battles and a short-lived rift between us. I had no tricks to pull out of my hat, except the determination to make everyone around me miserable.

Eventually my dad's decision would start my journey toward fulfillment and happiness . . . but at age fourteen, I didn't know that. And I didn't know that the decision to hate something before I'd even tried it was as simplistic as the story I'd loved as a kid, and that if I wanted to pursue my dreams, I'd have to grow up.

The Boogeyman

When I was a kid, I was afraid of the Boogeyman. He hid in the dark, lurked in the shadows and I don't know exactly what he looked like, but he was big and mean and very strong. One night, long after I thought I'd conquered that fear, I had a nightmare. In it, the Boogeyman was attacking me. I was with my best friend, running through the woods. It was very much like *The Blair Witch Project*—choppy, disorientating, and graphic. The dream slanted sideways, sometimes with the vision out of frame; black and white; blood red.

Suddenly I turned around and faced the monster. To this day I can't remember what he looked like, but he was huge. We fought for what seemed like forever. Sweat burned my eyes and blurred my vision. My arms and legs ached with the effort and strain. Eventually I chopped off the Boogeyman's head. I'm not sure how, I just did it.

The thing is, I didn't really believe in the Boogeyman at the time, but he was still in my dreams. Fear is like that. It's always lurking beneath the surface. All Olympic-level athletes experience it. My dream might have meant something, but at the time I didn't know what.

By the spring of 1996 I had won Overall for my age group in U.S. Short Track, a group title for U.S. Long Track, and was the North American Short Track Champion in my age group. There was an international competition being held at the same time as the North American Championship. The U.S. National Team and the Japanese team were squaring off in Red Deer, Canada. Never one to miss any opportunity, my dad sidled up to Jeroen Otter, the U.S. senior national head coach, and asked him for advice.

"I don't know what the next step is," my dad explained to Otter. "I don't want Apolo's career in short track to falter because I don't have the information necessary to help him."

Otter agreed that I was a promising skater, and told my dad that I should go to Lake Placid, New York, where the U.S. Junior National Development Team trains. There was one problem. I was only fourteen, and the residency program didn't start until age fifteen. But my father wasn't going to let my age stand in the way. He telephoned the Junior Development Team coach, Pat Wentland. They talked about my skating, race times, and wins, and about my potential. Pat decided that he really wanted me on the team. He met with the entrance committee and fought for me. The committee agreed to make an exception and allow me into the program, which was a year long, involved living in a dorm, training, and attending school. It began in June 1996. That's when my father experienced the second problem, and it was bigger than the first. I didn't want to go. No way.

In hindsight, I was afraid to leave my home and the life I knew. I was barely a teenager, loved my friends, and refused to even consider living at the training center. My summer vacation was already planned—camping, beaches, water parks, house parties, barbecues and more parties. I had places to go and people to see.

My father told me Lake Placid was the opportunity of a lifetime. "Chances don't come around every day and if you don't grab them, they never come back," Dad explained. "Everyone gets one big opportunity, not four or five, because that's the only way life can be fair to each person."

He was hitting me with the big stuff—playing for keeps. But my dad wasn't just sending me to train, he was taking me away from my buddies. He knew that 75 percent of them were good kids, but he also knew that I was fourteen and susceptible to negative influences. Dad wasn't going to allow me to get into trouble and if that meant sending me away, he'd be the bad guy. What I didn't understand back then was how much my father was going to miss me. All I knew was that he was trying to tear me away from home.

My father refused to drop the subject of Lake Placid. I was supposed to fly to New York in early June. By late June I was still home. It had become a battle, and then an all-out war. We fought all the time. He just kept saying I was going, easing up, and then coming at me again from a different angle. This is how it went:

"I'm not going to Lake Placid."

"This is your ticket to the 1998 Olympics."

"I don't care."

"There'll be older kids there and you like hanging out with older kids."

"I'm not going."

"The coach and team are already there, waiting for you."

"No."

"If you don't like it, you can come home. Just give it three months."

"I'm not going."

"It will be fun . . . a new place . . . you're going to go, period."

In late June, Dad literally packed my bags, put me in the car, and drove me to the airport. The ride was silent and the tension was thick. If anger was a brick wall, I'd built a house around myself with barbed wire. Dad walked me into the terminal, got my ticket and took me to the boarding gate. Then he made a mistake . . . he said good-bye, told me I'd be okay, and left me to board the plane alone. I had never planned to get on that flight.

I went to a payphone, called a buddy, and he picked me up at the airport. First we went to his house and dropped off my bags. Then we went to a party just like I'd planned to during the summer. Meanwhile, my father, who'd gone back to work, decided to stop by the airport on his way home to make sure I'd boarded and my flight was on its way to New York. Deep down, he thought there might be a problem. He learned at the gate that I'd never gotten on the plane.

For the next five days I went to fairs, the mall, parties, and movies. I had a plan—I'd stay with each of my friends for a few days, then move on before their parents figured out anything was wrong and called my dad. I was fourteen, had no money, but figured I could live that way for at least a year, maybe more because I had friends who lived all over Washington State. I was a kid trying to pull off the biggest act of rebellion in my life and I remember the exhilaration and the feeling that I was standing on the edge of a cliff, one foot in the air, about to step off.

I would sneak back home to get more clothes while my dad was working. I wasn't too slick about those visits. I could have borrowed clothes and never gone back, but as the days wore on, part of me was trying to get caught so that I could have a final confrontation with my dad. In addition I'd accidentally left a list of my friends and their telephone numbers in my bedroom. But it didn't matter at the time because I thought that I'd found a sanctuary and didn't have to do what he said anymore.

My father actually figured out where I was early on, but he decided to give me time to cool off before he drove over to my friend's house. He says it was one of the worst moments of his life. He had to ring the doorbell of someone else's home in order to see his son. My friend's mom hadn't even thought to call him to question why I was there or to alert him (I think she just thought I was on summer vacation). I was living in another family's house, and the moment crushed my dad.

When Dad asked to see me, I trudged into the front hallway and just stood there, shoulders hunched, head down, staring through hooded eyes at his outline in the bright doorway. The moment didn't seem real, more like a movie. At the time, he believed I was really in emotional trouble, but all he said was, "Apolo, you have to come home." I didn't budge and he left.

Dad knew that the decision to come home had to be mine, but he remembers thinking that he could relate to parents whose kids have been kidnapped and brainwashed by a cult. My face was completely blank and my eyes were cold and empty. It's not a moment I'm proud of and when he recalls it, there are tears in his eyes.

My dad called a female friend of the family for help. He believed that he'd reached a dead end but that I might listen to someone else, maybe a woman. While I wasn't hanging out with a gang member, he thought the particular friend I was staying with was a very bad influence and it scared him to realize how many forces were out there just waiting to grab me. I guess that's what parents have to go through all the time—the idea that even if they do their best, the world is filled with people who can hurt their child in tons of different ways.

A day after Dad came to get me, I packed my bags and went home. Not because of the female friend who spoke with me, but because I was scared of what my father might do. Truth is, I didn't really want to be on my own. In hindsight, I realize that my dad would never have given up on me, even if I hadn't come home within twenty-four hours (days, weeks, or years), but I was just a kid and I was afraid. When I walked through the front door of my house, the look on Dad's face was pure relief.

We talked a lot over the next week. Dad explained to me that no matter how tough a situation got, I could never again cut myself off from my family. "Your friends may be with you for a week, a month, a year, but in the end your family is the only thing that's permanent and I'm the one who will take care of you no matter what."

Still upset and angry, I knew deep down that my father was right. I might no longer believe in the Boogeyman, but there were things that still scared me. Losing my father's love and support were at the top of the list.

Thousands of Miles Away

The only way I'd ever be on the television show *Fear Factor* is if it was for a lot of money for a great charity. If you're not familiar with the show, a group of six "normal" people face a series of specific challenges that involve overcoming their greatest fears—like heights, rats, water, spiders, and enormous bugs.

The contestants constantly razz each other and it reminds me of my in-line skating days, when talking to psyche out your opponents was the norm and fun. I think I'd jump out of a plane or get in a boxing ring, but I don't like bugs, period. I could eat some termites, maybe a couple of maggots, but cockroaches are nasty, crawl between the cracks, carry all kinds of diseases, and live in places I don't want to imagine.

What strikes me most about that television program is that it doesn't begin to address my biggest fear: struggling. I fear struggling in my sport, life, and financially. It's the idea of never being comfortable or happy.

I didn't talk to my father on the plane ride to Lake Placid. I may have grudgingly agreed to go to New York, but I was still angry about leaving home. He understood that I didn't want to leave my home and friends, it hurt him to upset me, but he was also unwilling to let me blow a chance to train with the U.S. Junior Development Team. That meant he would personally deliver me to the training center. My dad put me in the front row and flew in the back. He figured we needed some time apart.

Lake Placid is in the middle of nowhere—what's called "Upstate New York." We couldn't even fly directly there; we had to change planes in Detroit, land in Albany, get a rental car, and then drive three hours. We traveled on winding roads, surrounded by tall pines and hills no longer snowcapped but brown and uninviting. The car ride was silent, except for the moments I'd tell my dad just how horrible he was. He agreed that the landscape was bleak but pointed out how clean the air was. I replied that it was clean in Seattle, too.

By the time we arrived at the training center, it was dark. But I could still see that there was no town, save a one-way street that wasn't wide enough for a truck to pass a car without pulling off on the shoulder. Lake Placid is a small village in the Adirondack Mountains. During the Great Depression it hosted the third Olympic Games in 1932, though only seventeen nations and 348 athletes showed, despite the new arena and bobsled run.

In 1980 Lake Placid made another successful bid for the Olympics and hosted the thirteenth Winter Games, which is hard to believe since the population of the town was only about 2700 people and organizers worried that the place was too small for the Games. Fifty million dollars was spent on snowmaking systems, ski jumps, additional ice rinks, new arenas, and an Olympic Village. The village is now a medium-security prison in Ray Brook, between Lake Placid and Saranac Lake, as per an agreement with the federal government in return for funding and support.

The only good thing I can write about Lake Placid is that it was the site where history was made by American speed skater Eric Heiden. He won a record five gold medals at the 1980 Olympics. It's also the site where the 1980 U.S. Olympic men's hockey team beat Russia on their way to capturing the gold medal.

* * *

Pat Wentland, then coach of the Junior National Team and all of the other athletes in training, greeted my father and me when we arrived at Lake Placid. *I have nothing in common with any of you,* I thought, looking them over. They were all from the East Coast and Midwest— places like Maryland and Ohio. *Give me a break and get away from me. I don't want to be here and I'm leaving really soon.* That night, in my dorm room single bed, I was not comfortable or happy.

The next morning my training began. My father and I went into "town" to buy a cheap road bike so that I could work out with the team. I remember that I did well, and Pat told my father that I could be one of the best skaters in the world. Dad stated that he was pessimistic about the chance of my staying.

Pat told my dad that everything was going to be okay.

"Apolo is not conservative or from the East Coast," my dad replied, looking around at all the other clean-cut skaters. "He's a West Coast kid."

Despite my bad attitude, I was drawn to Pat. A medium-built man with brownish-blond hair cut into a flattop, he exuded energy and the kids at the training center respected him. He was strict and intense, but rarely yelled and had a background skating short track. He was three-time National Short Track Champion, two-time North American Short Track Champion, World Team member, and placed fourth at the World Short Track Championships. Best of all, Pat trained side by side on and off the ice with his athletes. I was fourteen and had no formal training. Pat was my first real coach.

I compare every coach throughout my career to Pat. He's a man who knew how to turn me into a champion skater in one year, so his influence can't be minimized. Pat Wentland was a force in my life at age fourteen, a role model, and a constant inspiration. I respect and value his opinions to this day.

My father left Lake Placid a few days after we'd arrived, and I was pretty unhappy. I called my friends every day and while some thought I shouldn't blow the chance to skate and wished they had the same opportunity, most asked when I was coming home. "After three months," I'd reply. That's how long I'd promised my dad I'd stay: mid-July to mid-October.

Each week my father would call, but I'd pretend I was still angry. He'd tell me I was going to be okay, and I'd tell him that I hated everything, especially the food. Repetitive is the best way to describe how we ate. Monday, waffles, Tuesday, pancakes, Wednesday, French toast . . . week in and week out. Dinners were the same each day of the week too, especially the vegetables. Plus, I was tired and sore.

I'd never trained before, not like Lake Placid. We'd wake up at 7 A.M. and go for an hour run, then two hours skating followed by two hours of weights. I was six weeks behind the other kids in the program, so I had to work twice as hard to catch up. After a month, my body started to get used to the schedule. I lost some of my attitude about Lake Placid and I made my first real friend.

Donald Stewart was hilarious and the craziest kid I've ever known—hence his nickname, "Crazy-D." He had mad energy and was incredibly strong, and we became training partners and roommates. Donald hated it when other athletes thought they were better than he was, and when we'd run in the mornings, he'd sprint for the last half hour so that no one could catch or pass him. It would kill him, but he'd laugh the whole way and I'd stay with him because he was so funny. There were days, however, when we'd hang at the back of the pack, then peel off at the local pizza place, hitching a ride back to the center after we'd eaten our fill.

Despite the occasional slice of pizza, Crazy-D was driven to train. Some mornings he'd wake up at 3 A.M. just to do an extra workout.

And if he wasn't training, he was trying to scare everyone with pranks. That kid would waste five hours hiding under a dusty, nasty bed just for the chance to scare you. I was actually starting to have a great time at the training center because of Donald when school began.

The public school in Lake Placid is right next to the training center. In September I went to school from 10 A.M. until 3 P.M. and learning was sandwiched between morning and evening workouts. My class was only twenty-three kids and I couldn't avoid the watchful eyes of the teachers as I had in Seattle. But that's not why I hated the school. I hated it because I was bored and not at all entertained. There was no diversity—I didn't see any Latinos, and there were only two black kids and two Asians in the whole school. Everyone else was white, and though I'm a combination of Caucasian and Japanese, I've always considered myself Asian. I grew up surrounded by blacks, Latinos, and Asians, and I was stuck in a school where it seemed like everyone was somehow related, sitting at the same desks where their grandfathers had once been taught.

Gone were the metal detectors and security guards that had been part of the scenery of my childhood. I was used to seeing fights every single day after junior high school. They'd happen one block from my classes, on the same corner each day. None of the kids ever went to get a teacher.

I never fought, partially because my friends backed me up before things got out of hand and also because it frightened me. Sometimes I'd get called a name on the basketball court, but that didn't bother me because I'd already gotten out my aggression at practice.

I'm not saying I grew up in South Central L.A. We lived a half hour from Seattle, in a bedroom community called Federal Way. Back then, there were a lot of older people in our neighborhood. We lived in a three-bedroom, two-bathroom home. The walls and narrow hallways were lined with pictures of Dad and me. I had a lot of stickers in my bedroom and a poster of outer space and the planets, but I never wanted to be an astronaut or a fireman or a rock singer. I just wanted to hang out with my friends and it took a long time for me to develop any other goals, which sounds strange for an Olympian, but it's true.

Outside the front gates our neighborhood turned into apartments and over the years it became pretty tough and had fairly high petty crime rates. I remember passing by the fitness center down the street and seeing cars with bashed windows. Parked cars were an invitation in my neighborhood for vandalism and robbery, even at 6 A.M. when kids were walking to school. Looking at the shattered glass and graffiti I used to wonder why people had to do that. I understood the importance and value of my dad's car in our lives. Without it he couldn't get to work, take me to training, or travel with me to competitions. My dad's car was vandalized two times and it really upset me.

Contrary to my reactions to Lake Placid, and what the media reported during the 2002 Olympics, I was a good kid growing up. I hung out in Kent, Auburn, Tacoma, SeaTac, and Bellevue—wherever my friends lived. A few of my friends made the choice to join the Bloods or the Crips (gangs originating in L.A. with chapters all over the country), but I never rolled that way.

It sounds so threatening when you read the names, but the thing is every neighborhood has gangs, people just don't know about them. I never joined one because I was competing so much that I didn't feel the need—like I said, I got out my aggressions in the pool or skating rink.

I respect the idea that your gang is your family and that they watch out for you. Some kids really need the protection. But in the end it seems to me that it's more about making money to try to get out of your neighborhood and get a better life. Fortunately skating was my way out. Believe it or not, my friends never pressured me and I was able to hang out with just about anyone from both sides without problems.

I was a fish out of water in Lake Placid. But the thing about kids is that they can get used to anything. Surrounded by athletes and achievers, I went with the current. And I have to say that's what my father was hoping, even though he couldn't have known that forcing me to go to Lake Placid would have any positive results. In fact, he thought that after three months I'd come back home. While I was "upstate," my father was trying to figure out a way to keep me busy in Seattle and away from any negative influences if I left the training center. He still believes to this day that if I hadn't started to excel in Lake Placid and I'd come home, I might have ended up in trouble.

The truth is that I don't know. I was only fourteen when I left home. After the 1996-1997 season of short track, I would return to Seattle for a few months, and maybe I thought that was going home at the time, but it really wasn't. I didn't fully understand then that you carry the people you love wherever you travel and that home is just a building.

Within a month of training at Lake Placid, it seemed obvious that I was becoming one of the best on the team. Pat's style as a coach was so enthusiastic and passionate that he triggered my belief in myself. Plus he was working out with everyone side by side, feeling the pain. I was getting really fast, and one day I asked him what would happen if I improved *too* fast. Being only fourteen, this is what the conversation sounded like:

"Pat, what if I get really good . . . I mean, I'm only fourteen . . ."

"What are you talking about?" Pat asked.

"I might burn out and be out of the picture," I explained.

Pat very seriously told me that wouldn't be the case.

"Okay, then, I want you to make me a machine. I want to be the best ever. Make me a machine."

❊ ❊ ❊

In late August 1996 my father returned to Lake Placid to visit me. The training center was also hosting a World Cup and had inserted a special event called the "Junior Exhibitions." I'd only had six weeks of training, but Pat chose me as one of the skaters to represent the United States. It was my debut as a Junior National Team member and I felt like all eyes were going to be on me, the new kid, to see if I was any good. I was excited and best of all, my dad would get to watch me skate.

The junior race was set for a Saturday. That Tuesday I fell at the end of practice. The Zamboni used to clean the ice had been brought in from outside and had dropped some sand on one of the corners. When I dug into the ice, the grains stripped the edge of my blade. I went down and hit the wall so hard that it knocked my hip out of joint. There was intense pain, and then numbness. I tried to get up but couldn't walk because my entire leg was completely locked. A trainer helped me off the ice and put my hip back into joint. My father came over to tell me that things were going to be okay—there would be other races. I told him I could recover in time for the exhibition. No one believed me.

By Saturday, I still had trouble walking. I got on the ice anyway, and while the other skaters zoomed around the track, I skated slowly, trying to warm up. I felt tight, and hot licks of pain radiated from my hip joint. *Breathe,* I told myself, *just breathe.* To this day I don't know how I found the strength to compete. When I got on the starting line, surrounded by great skaters, I just rose to their level. I was in the zone, feeling no pain or doubt, and by the end of the day, I'd won the exhibition and everyone knew my name.

The Rock

There's a Greek myth about a guy named Sisyphus. Nearing death, Sisyphus decided to test his wife's love and he told her to place his unburied body in the middle of the public square. When Sisyphus woke up, he was dead and in the underworld. Pissed off that his wife had actually put him in the square and that the exposure probably led to a faster death, Sisyphus got the permission of Pluto, god of the underworld, to go back up to Earth so that he could yell at his wife.

Once he was back on Earth, in the sunlight, Sisyphus didn't want to go back to the darkness of death. So he ran away, hid from Pluto, and lived for years on the edge of an ocean where he could see the water and the mountains. Another god, Mercury, decided that he couldn't let Sisyphus cheat death so he dragged him back down to the underworld.

As punishment for his actions, Sisyphus was forced to spend eternity pushing an enormous boulder up a hill, straining and sweating the entire way. When he reached the top, he had to watch the boulder roll back down and then repeat the process . . . forever.

I was so fired up by the time I got to the January 1997 Junior World Trials that I was certain I was going to make the team, travel around the world, and become a great skater. The competition was held in Milwaukee, Wisconsin, and from the moment I took my guards off and stepped onto the ice, my blades felt bad.

Every race, I constantly work on the bend of my blades with a radius gauge down to ten-thousandths of a hair. In addition, the rocker (which allows you to turn on a dime if it's right) also needs to be altered, depending on the bend, the sharpness of the blade, the type of ice, and how I'm skating on a particular day. When a skate is right, you know it. In Milwaukee, my skate felt off.

The problem was, no one could figure out exactly what was wrong. Pat and my dad, who'd come all the way to Milwaukee to watch me race, tried to fix my blades, but couldn't. I didn't have any spares so I had to do the warm-up with bad blades. While all the other skaters sped around the track, I went carefully because I felt like I couldn't hold on to the ice in the corners. After warm-up, I skated right into the events, which is dangerous, because I could have ended up injured.

In the 1000-meter time trial I pushed through the problem and broke the U.S. record, but the only race I made it into the finals for was the 1000-meters. I won that event, but came in third overall and didn't make the junior's cut because they take only the top two U.S. skaters for the international team. My dad drove back to Lake Placid with me. It was the biggest defeat of my young life and I was depressed. I felt like I'd given up my summer, my friends, and my life in Seattle for nothing.

"You did a wonderful job, Apolo," my dad said. "Even with something wrong with your blade, you've proven you can still perform."

"Yeah, right," I sarcastically replied.

"You didn't quit, did you? You could have fallen and gotten injured, right?"

"I guess so."

"You should be proud. You won the one thousand-meter with a bad blade."

I started to enjoy the drive with my dad through the snow-covered mountains. The air did seem a little fresher and cleaner than Seattle's.

I returned to training with a vengeance. When Pat came back from traveling with the junior team, we talked again about working harder to improve my skating and he taught me one of the most important techniques I know. We were doing one-lap time trials and I went super hard. My time was 9.3 seconds. Pat told me to go again, but this time to just relax into it and go tighter around the corners. My time was 9.1 seconds. Two-tenths drop in time is huge in short track. Ahhh, the fine line between trying too hard and just flowing.

Listening has never been my strong point. It's something I work on to this day, but I tend to reinvent the wheel. I've been told I'm stubborn, but I grew up with a father who is tough as nails. Dad is one of those people who passionately believes he is almost always right. If we ever disagree, it's a mess. My dad can turn into a stone when we argue and it's like I'm talking to him through a glass window but he can't hear my voice. If Dad was Sisyphus, he'd push that boulder up every day, happy each time he'd succeeded in reaching the top, and determined when it rolled back down to push it up again, and this time to figure out a way to make it stay. No one would be able to talk him out of it. No one.

I came back to Lake Placid after not making the juniors determined to improve. I really wanted to perform well and started pushing hard. I was hungry to win, and because skaters who are age eligible can compete on both the junior and senior level, I set my sights on the March 1997 Senior World Trials. The senior team took five skaters, and back then the top two guys skated in the individual World Cup races and the remaining two joined them for the relay. The fifth guy on the team was the alternate.

The senior trials were an unbelievable experience. I raced against top guys like Tony Goskowicz and Andrew Gabel, who is a four-time Olympian. Gabel competed in speed skating when it was a demonstration sport at the 1988 Games, won seven medals at the Winter World University Games, and was a member of the U.S. long track team before moving on to short track in 1989. I mean, this guy was one of the best skaters in the U.S. I beat Gabel at the trials.

I won the nine-lap time trial that separates the top sixteen from the rest of the skaters. The next big race was a four-lap trial. I almost won that, too, but slipped on the last corner. I fell onto my chest but somehow managed to regain my feet before I hit the wall. Even when I started to slip, I knew I was going to pull something crazy off. When you're off, you fall and immediately hit the wall. Bam, it's over, and you feel the impact from the top of your head to your toes. Sometimes it knocks your breath out and you struggle to gasp in air. At the seniors, I knew I was on my blades. I could hear the crowd draw in its breath and then cheer when I crossed the finish line and tied for third. I was a warrior.

I was ranked first going into the races as the result of both the nine- and four-lap time trials. In the finals I won the 1500-meters, didn't place in the 1000-, came in second in the 3000-, and took fourth in the 500-meters. The way the point system worked, I technically had to race my last event but even if I didn't get any points for placing, I'd still won the U.S. Overall title and made the Senior World Team. That meant I was going to train with Jeroen Otter and the Senior National Team in Colorado. I'd be number one of the two U.S. skaters to race in the World Cup competitions—the other was Andrew Gabel.

I credit my win to a lot of things. I was a serious contender before I even stepped onto the ice. In Lake Placid I'd clocked in some incredible lap times that already had the seniors wondering who I was before I got to the trials. I was less than 150 pounds so I might not have looked threatening, but I had a tremendous amount of accumulated cross training. At the time of the '97 trials, many athletes still didn't understand the value of cross training and some hadn't incorporated anything more than running and weights into their programs. I'd been swimming for six years, and roller-skating, which because of the friction of the wheels is great resistance training. Plus years of in-line built a lot of endurance. Other skaters would be exhausted after 3000 meters of training, but I could do five times that distance on roller skates so I was in awesome shape, and especially hungry after the Junior World Trials.

Number one. In less than a year I made it to the top of short track, and was ranked number one on the U.S. senior team. Nobody had ever excelled in the sport that quickly. There are steps to take and most long and short track skaters have been training since they were three years old. They've had plenty of ice time and come from strong skating clubs. They understand training, equipment management, and how to travel throughout the world. What's more, they've known each other for years. After less than a year on the junior team, I was not part of the inner circle, and even after the senior trials were over, the then-president of the speed skating association didn't come over to meet me or shake my hand.

I said good-bye to the junior team, my friends at the training center, and Lake Placid, and flew to the Colorado Springs Olympic Training Center to begin the next stage of my career. There was no time for adjustment. Once in Colorado Springs I started training with the senior team. Otter, the head coach, had never trained a fourteen-year-old before. I was grouped with fifteen older men and women skaters who had previously trained under Otter. It was a case of too many skaters, no assistant coach to help Otter out, and no workouts designed specifically for my bones, muscles, or body type. It was unrealistic to think that I could lift like an eighteen-year-old athlete. In hindsight, I was destined for problems.

Even though I was the number-one skater on the team, there was no time spent or effort made to figure out what I needed to succeed as an athlete and competitor. There was no nutritional plan (I ate cold pizza, candy, whatever was in my tiny fridge when I was hungry), and no sports psychologist to help me adjust or just survive through the first few months. I'd lived away from home for almost a year, but at the junior level there was much more attention paid to what each skater needed to thrive, and coach Pat Wentland understood how to work with younger athletes.

When you are number one on the U.S. team, you immediately inherit the responsibility of competing at the World Cup level. There are six World Cup events around the globe plus the World Cup Championships in March of each year. I'd been in the upper echelons for ten months, but had never needed to travel the world, competition after competition. I lacked the stamina for international travel. It's not just about packing your bags and taking care of all the equipment needs before a trip. There are thirty-hour flights, acclimation to different climates and time changes—and there're only a few days when you arrive in places like Asia and Europe to prepare, train, and compete. Train, pack, travel, compete, fly home, train, pack . . . over and over again. Life was a blur.

I flew to my first World Championship after making the number-one spot on the team in that spring of 1997. It was held in Nagano, Japan, at the brand-new arena and rink that had been built for next year's Nagano Olympic Games. Everyone at the World Championships intimidated me—the Canadians, Chinese, Italians, Japanese, and of course the Korean team. I once again had blade problems. At the time, the blade of my old skate was riveted to a top tube and because I tend to pressure a blade extremely hard around the corners, it couldn't hold the pressure and came loose. I needed a new blade and made the switch to a fellow teammate's spare pair, but the rocker wasn't quite right. I was used to depending on my friends, fellow skaters, and coaches during competitions, but I didn't have any close friends on the national team, didn't know the other skaters well, and Otter was extremely busy trying to be everything to everyone. I needed a mechanic to help me and teach me how to care for my blades, but there wasn't one available for the underfunded short track team.

Competing internationally is a different world than national competitions. The skaters have a different style, intensity, endurance, and strength. They never seem tired. *Never.* They're taught to hide every weakness and they do a *great* job at it. Plus, they skate a much tighter radius. I remember wondering at Nagano where all the space between skaters was and I was really intimidated by the proximity of the other skaters. It's always hard to pass during races, but at Nagano it seemed impossible to fit through the tiny gaps without colliding and causing accidents.

I didn't make it to the 1500-meter final, was eliminated in the 1000-, and didn't advance to the 3000- final. Basically I got smoked every race and placed nineteenth overall. I left Nagano disillusioned and exhausted. I was tired of feeling like Sisyphus, and I decided with the infinite wisdom of a fourteen-year-old simply not to push the boulder up the hill anymore.

I lost sight of my goals in the spring of 1997. Drained after months of competitions and the pressures of living on my own and taking care of every aspect of my sport, I didn't want to train anymore. I missed my friends; I needed a break; I wanted to take the summer off. Neither my father nor I understood that my training couldn't be interrupted if I wanted to compete at the senior level. We both thought I could use a vacation and Dad wanted to make sure I continued to have some balance in my life—it was a crazy summer. But the playing field had changed.

Nationals for in-line skating are always in August, so an athlete's physical ability needs to peak in the summer. Short track is different—the season runs June through March, and normally there is no long summer break. While short track skaters can ease up for the months of June and July, they must continue to train if they're going to peak January through March for the World Championships and the Olympics.

I didn't train from April until almost August. My typical daily schedule was: Get up around 9 A.M. Have breakfast, call up one of my buddies and go over to his house around 10 and hang out until 3 at the beach. Dinner involved bbq's or pizza, a movie, and then a party at someone's house or just straight kickin' back. I didn't get on the ice once and later learned that no ice time means quickly losing the "feel" of the ice. There's no way to replace that feeling and it takes a long time to get it back.

By August 1997, just five months before the January 1998 Olympic Trials, I was in bad shape. Otter had told me to bike while home and put in lots of miles and I hadn't. Nor had I lifted weights, skated, stretched a muscle, or watched my diet—a bad combination of not working out, junk food, and puberty. I was fifteen pounds overweight when I went to a training camp in Chamonix, France, with the rest of my teammates, and I was the only guy who hadn't biked all summer.

I couldn't beat anybody up at the camp—I got smoked on everything. My lungs burned on the bike rides through the hillsides of France, my legs burned during practices, my weights were lower than the other skaters and when we ran, I was in the back of the pack. Plus, I got the flu. It got so bad that my coaches had a doctor come see me.

Otter suggested that I go home and that I would be okay if I rode my bike hard for two and a half weeks before returning to Colorado Springs to get ready for the next six competitions and the Olympic Trials. I went home and didn't train at all. There was a mountain in front of me, but I just sat down, ate a fat cheeseburger, and didn't even try to climb it.

Many of the skaters who had never really accepted that I was number one on the team were waiting for me when I returned to the Olympic Training Center. I was in trouble, physically and emotionally, and you know what happens to the weakest wolf in the pack. They went after me and I had no endurance, strength, or mental edge to protect myself.

Revival

Getting my ass kicked in Chamonix didn't affect me like it should have. In hindsight, I truly didn't get how much effort would be needed in getting ready for the Olympic Trials. I didn't comprehend the time and energy necessary to win any international event. I believed that if I tried my best every race, I would do well. I didn't understand the preparation part. As a result, the trials for the Olympics in Nagano were an enormous disappointment and nearly signaled the end of my skating career.

In the fall of 1997 I returned to Colorado Springs and forced myself once again to train hard. I started to take creatine, a legal muscle enhancer said to improve high-powered performance and increase muscle and fat-free mass. Creatine monohydrate is an amino acid that naturally occurs in the body and is concentrated in skeletal muscles. It's essential for the production of adenosine triphosphate (ATP), the major energy-storage molecule of the body. Muscles rely on creatine to help restore their supply of ATP after workouts.

Athletes using creatine sometimes find that they have less muscle fatigue in high-intensity exercises and can lift more weights. In '97 a lot of skaters were taking the enhancer to become more explosive off the starting line. My body reacted to the supplement immediately and I gained seven pounds and initially felt stronger. Unfortunately, over the next month the creatine began to have the opposite effect, making me sluggish while adding even more pounds.

I kept traveling to international competitions, but each time I returned it was harder and harder to recover from the strain. I got sick again and had to take another dose of antibiotics. I had no time to rest or get organized or sit down and evaluate my skating and the races. I lived in a tiny room with half-packed bags and dirty laundry and my schedule was chaotic. I felt like a chicken with its head cut off—running around without sight or direction. I needed help, but I didn't know how to say that to my coach and at the time I honestly didn't care that much.

My dad tried to step in because he realized by our irregular phone calls that I wasn't able to manage my time. He wanted to help me organize my blades, boots, and spare equipment, but he was too far away and I was in too deep a hole. Meanwhile I had a bull's-eye on my back and skaters were gunning for me every race. I felt depressed and negative about short track, my teammates, my abilities, and my desire to continue with the sport.

In December I went to the U.S. Junior Short Track Championship. I was still sick and should have withdrawn, but my coaches thought I should go, and I wasn't communicating my needs well or being vocal about my health. I was fifteen at the time, and it's hard to stand up to authority figures, especially coaches, during that age of uncertainty. I made the team, coming in second overall, but looking back, my coaches were shortsighted in their approach to my career. I needed to save up my strength and energy for the Olympic Trials, which frankly were more important. As a result of the wear and tear on my mind and body, I felt defeated long before I went to the trials.

The Olympic Trials that year were held in January 1998 over a two-week period, with competitions on Friday, Saturday, and Sunday, with the weekdays off to rest. My fighting spirit kicked in and I struggled to regain focus and power, but my body and mind were too fatigued to recognize the call.

There was a nine-lap time trial the first weekend, with points from the trial adding to points from the events. I hadn't done many time trials that year (I used to do them every two weeks with Pat), and by the time I'd finished the ninth lap, I was seeing stars and white dots burst across my line of vision. Needless to say, I received no points. I also didn't qualify for any of the weekend's finals.

The following weekend there was a four-lap time trial. The same thing happened. While my shocked father watched from the stands, I failed to make the remaining finals. Between races my dad would offer encouragement and suggest I watch some videotapes of skating to improve my performance. I just pushed him away. I didn't want to talk to anyone.

After the trials ended and I'd placed dead last (sixteenth of sixteen competitors), I saw Pat Wentland and told him that I'd probably skated my last race ever and planned to quit.

Shocked, Pat asked what I was talking about.

The look of confusion, concern, and disappointment on my father's face flashed through my mind. "I don't think my dad wants to support me anymore," I said. "This year was a waste." I was so disappointed in myself and embarrassed.

Pat told me to go home, do some training, and think about it before I made any decisions.

But I'd already made up my mind.

"Apolo was more than disappointed, he was devastated, and I was really worried that he was going to be wiped out of the sport."

That's what my dad said after the trials. It's true. I was broken down physically and emotionally. The competition had been traumatic for my dad, too. "You were like a weak lion chased by a pack of hyenas," Dad said. "You were bleeding and breathing hard and they attacked and tried to finish you off." My dad was furious at the coaches and the skating federation for what he saw as their failure of me. Dad believed they'd had a responsibility to help me adjust at the senior level. I was a young teen and talented skater, and I needed an investment of their time and consideration. But instead everyone around me wanted me to compete, compete, compete, and never tried to protect me or reach out with any true help. I was harder on myself. I believed it had been *my* failure to focus and train. *I* was responsible.

My dad decided that his first responsibility was to get me away from the sport of short track. He told the coaches he wasn't sure he'd allow me to come back, even though they wanted me to be on the World team. "Maybe this is the end of short track," he said, "maybe you can go back to swimming."

Swimming? Forget that! All I know is that I didn't feel like the lion he'd described me as, even a wounded one. My dad decided that he would take me to an isolated place where the media, my coaches, other skaters, or friends couldn't reach me. Total quiet, he said, was what I needed so that I could think about my life. We flew into Seattle and immediately drove up to the cottage at Iron Springs Resort.

The coast of Washington during the winter is a bleak, rainy, and strangely beautiful place. The drive from Seattle was quiet. We traveled in silence, knowing that each of us understood the importance of this trip. When we arrived at Iron Springs, sheets of rain buffeted the car. The sand was cold, the ocean looked rough and was freezing, and the skyline appeared to be a solid shade of gray.

There's no cable, telephone, or stereo in the cottage, but we brought a VCR, a small television, and skating tapes. We also brought a stationary bike, in case I felt like exercising without getting wet, and my cat, Tiggie, for company because my dad wouldn't be staying. My father filled the fridge with food and frozen dinners, and told me to call him from the pay phone down the road whenever I wanted to talk or was ready to come home.

"Think about your future," my dad advised. "Apolo, short track is not the only thing you can do. Figure out if skating should be in your life. If not, decide what you want." My father understood everything that I'd been through. If I no longer wanted to skate, fine, but the bottom line was that he didn't want me going home mindless. There was no right or wrong answer or direction, just a choice to be made to *keep moving*.

When I was young, my dad and I spent summers walking along the coastal beach, renting scooters and going swimming. But there was nothing to do at Iron Springs during the winter. Plus, I didn't have a car and town was a twenty-five-minute walk in the pouring rain. When Dad left the cottage I felt isolated and alone. The first night I went to sleep early, hunkering down beneath the blankets, trying to shut out the world. When I woke, it was still raining and the sky had not changed its charcoal color. The storm outside was rattling the windowpanes, but it was also inside me, and there was nowhere to hide.

I stayed at the cottage for nine long days. Surrounded by the gloom and silence, all I could do *was* think. I started to bike, pedaling away the hours inside the small living room, trying to escape from myself but going nowhere. The first two days were endless. On the third day I decided to start a journal:

Day 3 Dialogue
1-21-98, after the Olympic Trials

9:15 A.M. Got up. It was very cold so I cranked up all of the heaters. Tiggie was sleeping in my bed, nice and comfortable. I made juice consisting of yogurt, one banana, carrots, orange juice, and broccoli. I had two bowls of cereal, one bowl was with blueberries. Built fire and ate right next to it. Made Tiggie some toys to play with while I ate.

10:30 A.M. Started to write in daily journal and thought, I want to go and jog today between the worst rain. While watching Tiggie play I noticed that she always makes me smile.

10:40 A.M. If I come back and try to skate at the World Team Trials, my goal is to be able to skate at 150 pounds, and to be very lean, with no muscle loss. I need to work on my endurance, jogging and cycling. I want to be more agile on my skates. I need to watch videos of other skaters and I need to work on my dry-land technique.

If I do skate at World Team Trials I am skating to WIN, not second, not third, but FIRST and only that. If my dad helps me and I keep faith in God, myself, and my dad, I think I can do it. If for some reason I can't do it, then I know at least one very important special thing. I gave something 110 percent. If I could do that I believe I'd be one of the top skaters in the world.

12:20 P.M. I'm going for a walk outside, even though it's raining. . . .

I ventured outside. There wasn't a soul on the beach. I thought about calling my dad and having him pick me up, but I didn't have anything to say yet. I jogged for ten minutes back to the cottage and spent the afternoon watching skating videos. When I couldn't stand to be inside any longer, I took off for an hour run.

5:00 P.M. My run was intense. I am very bored and pretty lonely right now and wish I had someone to talk to or that Dad would come up and visit me. I very truly believe that I can make my goals, but I need to SKATE and be coached on my technique. Without skating it is very idiotic to even try this goal. I want to give my goal

110 percent every day because I know I'm capable of that and it would help tremendously when I train.

5:10 P.M. Watch more tapes and take a shower. . . .

I began to train three times a day—I'd go for a run in the morning along dark, incredibly steep, curving roads. There were no cars and I pounded along the asphalt in the crappy sneakers I'd brought, pushing past the discomfort of the hills and my aching feet. I ran for hours.

When I returned to the cottage, I'd bike away the afternoon, then watch videos of skating, over and over again, focused on every minute detail. In the evenings I would run again. The rain never stopped, I was in pain because I was out of shape, and soaking wet because I didn't have the right clothing with me. It felt like the rain penetrated my skin and was trickling through my blood and seeping into my bones. I was constantly wet, damp, and cold. I mindlessly trained each day and night until I was half dead, had shin splints, sore feet, and fat blisters.

Day 4 Dialogue
1-22-98

8:30 A.M. Got up and made eggs with cheese, toast, and blended juice.

9:20 A.M. Just finished breakfast and I want to go run at 10:30 until 12:30 P.M., a two-hour run. Pray time . . . "Dear Heavenly Father . . . Thank you for giving me the opportunity to be here. It is very lonely and I would like to go back home. I have started training hard again. Will you help me keep on training so I can give my goal 110 percent? Pray by Jesus' name. Amen."

9:50 A.M. Watch tapes, then run.

One day while training and dead tired, I just stopped on the side of the road. An enormous flat boulder perched over the Pacific. In the downpour I sat on the rock. *What am I doing?* I asked myself. *What am I doing? Do I really want to sacrifice the next four years for short track? Do I want to make the next Olympic team? There's no money in the sport so why am I doing it? There's no recognition or stardom. I'll never get famous from short track. So why put in the time and effort and go through pain?* The only answers I received were the steady patter of rain, the cold ocean wind, and the taste of my own sadness.

I knew that if I got up from that boulder and didn't continue my run, I'd never competitively skate again. It was either keep running or walk back to the cottage and call my father to pick me up. I asked myself the same question over and over again. *Why am I doing this?* And the only answer I could find was that I love skating. I mean I really love doing it. I prayed to God asking Him to give me strength to be strong and push through the tough times. I asked to be able to become a great athlete. And then I got up and started running.

"I want to skate."

"Apolo, are you sure that's what you want to do?"

"I want to skate."

I hung up the payphone and made my way back to the cottage, jumping over puddles, to wait for my father. Nine days after he'd dropped me off in Iron Springs, he came back to retrieve me. Everything had changed. My career had both ended and begun anew. I recognized that I was talented and had a gift. I realized that I loved my sport. And I also understood for the first time in my life that I couldn't accomplish everything alone. I'd known that it took coaches to help, but now I really got that it takes a team to transform someone with raw talent into a champion—coaches, sports trainers, friends, and fans. Most of all it takes the consistency of always having someone in your corner.

After that trip to the cottage my father became my true partner in short track. He'd always been there, steering me away from trouble, supporting me, driving me to competitions, cheering from the stands, but I'd been unwilling to completely depend upon his help. On the car drive home from the cottage, my dad pledged his continued support. "I'm going to jump on the wagon and I will be your Olympic 2002 team partner."

Now the question was, where to train while waiting for the coaches in Colorado Springs to return from the February 1998 Olympics in Nagano, Japan.

"Well, I think you can train at Lake Placid through the Olympics and maybe get ready for the 1998 World Cup Team Trials there."

Lake Placid . . . again. *Sigh.* "Okay."

I flew to Lake Placid a few days later. I decided to try a new junior coach, John Monroe, and he was excited to train me. There was another skater training for the Worlds at the same time, a friend named Mike Kooreman, who also hadn't made the Olympic team. The first week I arrived I had trouble getting back into the groove of training, but Mike was focused on making the Worlds, and his enthusiasm caught on. Back then, in order to make the team I'd have to skate against everyone who'd made the Olympics. It doesn't work that way anymore—if you make the Olympic Team, you automatically have a place on the World Team. But in 1998 I'd have to fight my way to the top yet again. If I didn't make the team, I would probably quit for good.

I started pushing my body to the limit. I'd run, lifted weights, and done a crazy bike workout—ninety minutes on the bike doing sprints and interval training (thirty second sprints, rest, forty-five second sprints, rest, minute sprints, rest, over and over again). It doesn't sound like it's that long, but it's a hell workout. No one can sprint the entire time—it's impossible. You leave the bike with nothing but the fact that you finished.

One day I felt lightheaded and saw spots, but I pushed through it. When I got off the bike I almost fainted. I was training in the sports medicine facility and needed to get back to my room and hydrate. Mike saw me a few minutes later. He told me that I had lain down in the hallway and passed out.

John Monroe was worried that I was pushing too hard and over-training. I'd come to Lake Placid still tired from the Olympic Trials and the year. The World Team Championship was in March and I didn't have a lot of time to get ready, so I'd go for extra runs, and do third training sessions alone. I refused to listen to John's advice. I was fifteen and determined to get back to the top level of short track.

Nothing was going to stand in my way.

Concentration

If fate means you to lose, give him a good fight.

—William McFee

I saw spots at the end of the first time trial. It was just like I'd felt after training on the bike in Lake Placid. The March 1998 Senior National Championship in Marquette, Michigan was going to be a waste. That's what I was afraid of on the first day of the competition—all that hard work going down the drain. The championships were extremely important because the World Team members would be chosen and decisions would be made about who was eligible to compete in the 1998-1999 World Cup events.

I wore my game face—quiet and unexpressive. Inside I was jittery and tight. I skated well, competitive in every race, and was good enough to be in the running to make the team. It came down to the last race—a 3000-meter event. I had to beat two skaters to make the team. One of them was a pure endurance athlete and the 3000- was his race. We all got off the line well. I tried to be patient, hang in the back of the pack and conserve my energy, but when the two skaters in my sights took off, I had to follow so that the gap between us wouldn't get too wide. The race was a blur, but in the end I beat them both.

I got the fifth and last spot on the team. The top two skaters get to compete in all the individual events, plus four guys get to skate the relay. Position number five meant I was an alternate so I wouldn't get to compete in many of the World Team races. But that was okay, I told myself, at least I'd be there.

We traveled to Austria and my coach allowed me to skate as a member of the 5000-meter relay. We did well, but for me that wasn't the point. I had become used to skating every event; being number one; carrying the most weight for the team. All of a sudden I was watching other skaters take what I'd thought of as my place. Even though being the alternate provided me with important rest time, I didn't like it. I couldn't stand being number five—the last guy on the team—the least valuable skater. I'd cheated the fate I'd been afraid was mine, the fire was there and I once more wanted to be a machine.

I went back to Seattle for three months because until I was feeling confident and strong, I didn't want to be in Colorado Springs. It was part embarrassment on my behalf, part game plan, and a psychological ploy to both make myself feel better and not let other skaters know my weaknesses. Once a competitive athlete sees their adversary is in trouble, they're tougher, stronger, and better just by virtue of their perceived beliefs.

My dad and I went out and bought a better stationary bike and a little television. We set up a gym in the garage. I trained by myself on the bike two hours a day, riding hard, dripping sweat with a small fan blowing warm air over me. I'd watch videos while I rode, analyzing everything about my technique and my competitors'.

Using anger and young fire, I trained through the pain. I ran three times a week at my old high school track. When my dad came home from work we'd do dry-land exercises in the parking lot of the local high school and then drive to a fifteen-mile park trail so my dad could ride his bike alongside me while I'd in-line. He'd try to chase me down, and once almost broke his leg racing me across a railroad track.

I was too fast for him to catch. While I was missing ice time by training at home, I struck a balance in resistance training and dry-land workouts.

I was invited by my friends to hang out, but I was training so hard and was so into it, that I didn't go to many parties. When I did go out, I'd come home early by choice. I cut every single ounce of fat out of my diet. If I ate lasagna, I'd push the cheese off my plate. Over those two months my endurance levels and my strength from riding and in-lining shot up. I was losing weight and getting lean, but I was also getting really strong. I read a lot of books on nutrition to improve my diet and spent time talking to my dad about skating and getting pumped up. Our relationship at the time was great—Dad saw me training hard and he was really happy I'd rededicated myself to the sport.

It wasn't the only challenge I took on at the time. I also wanted to finish high school. With constant travel, I hadn't been able to keep up in Seattle. Once I moved to Colorado Springs, the only high school I could attend was a twenty-minute walk each way in the snow, wind, and cold of the Rocky Mountains. I didn't have a car or the time to commute because everyday practices got in the way.

In the spring of 1998, amid training, I tried to enroll at my local high school, Decator. It was too late to transfer, so they enrolled me in the Internet Academy. I can't say enough about the help I received from Decator to find a program that worked for me. The Internet Academy isn't just a correspondence course, it's much more intense. There's constant contact between teachers and students, learning CDs, and the pace is as slow or as fast as each individual needs.

For me, taking classes online was the perfect solution. You have to be self-motivated because it's easy to put off taking tests, but that was never a problem for me. By returning to high school studies, I also felt a surge of self-confidence that I didn't get from short track. Education has always been important to me. While there are classes I didn't like, I never considered not getting my high school diploma.

After a few months training at home, it was time to get back on the ice, and I returned to Colorado Springs feeling like I was strong enough to be with the team and compete. "Did you lose weight? You look lean." That's what my fellow skaters said when I returned. I just smiled and shrugged. I saw Mike Kooreman and we went for a run—my first one at altitude after three months at sea level. Mike was in awesome shape, really at his peak at the time, and he pushed hard. I stayed with him for the entire run, and I felt good . . . really good.

By the time I went for a training ride with the team and the newly appointed head coach, Pat Wentland, everyone knew I'd come back incredibly strong. I led the entire ride and even though Pat told me to slow down on the hills, I was just riding easy, not pushing myself at all. The rest of the team drafted off me the entire time, and there was a strong headwind going up the hills, but I was still dropping people. At the end of the ride I saw in Pat's eyes that it was going to be a good year.

That summer something else in my career changed too. I met Dave Creswell. A student at Colorado College, Dave had some great professors who developed his interest in sports psychology. With the Olympic Training Center so close to his college, he had the opportunity to work with athletes from his freshman year on. Captivated by the idea of improving performance and quality of life, Dave let all of his professors and everyone at the training center know that he was interested in working with the athletes.

Pat Wentland, who believed in the value of sports psychology, and also wanted someone around to make sure his team got to bed on time, invited Dave to become a resident adviser for the short track team. He would be able to learn, advise, and help the skaters, with the understanding that he was not a psychologist yet and any real problems should be directed to a medical professional. Pat's idea was a good one, especially since Dave was only slightly older than the members of the team (we ranged in age from fifteen to twenty-one and he was twenty-one), and would be accepted as part of our generation—a peer. We might, Pat hoped, actually listen to Dave.

Dave enrolled in summer school classes so that he could take the first semester of his junior year off. He moved into the dorms in August. At first his role was simply social support. He's a great athlete and was on his college tennis team, so he always watched practices and workouts with the short track men's and women's teams. Very slowly he introduced the idea of goal setting, giving skaters logbooks to record their goals, thoughts, and experiences. About 10 percent of the skaters were excited by the idea and used the books. The rest completely rejected the idea. I rejected the idea.

I didn't see the need for goal setting or a diary. Plus when I meet someone new it takes a while for me to trust him. I noticed the fact that Dave wasn't going anywhere, he was part of the furniture, so deep down I wondered if he was someone I might be able to count on in the future. I started to acknowledge his presence—just "Hi, how are you doing," no big conversations. I still didn't use the logbook (to this day it's a point on which Dave and I disagree). Sitting down and recording my thoughts just doesn't work for me. But one day Dave and I decided to play badminton, and luckily, it was the avenue through which Dave was finally able to reach me.

The U.S. Olympic Badminton Team practices at the Colorado Olympic Training Center, so they have courts set up. I'd work out six hours a day, then meet Dave for two hours of badminton. I had never played before but immediately loved the speed and athletics of the sport, and also the mental challenges. Since Dave's a tennis player and good at all racquet sports, he'd beat me. But even after a day of training I had a seemingly unlimited reserve of energy and a desire to learn. Eventually I got good enough to win.

On the court Dave and I developed a mutual respect based on athletics and training. Always subtle, Dave used opportunities during our games to point out why he would win several points in a row against me. He probed to find out what caused my lapses of focus and I started to have a deeper awareness of my own mental dialogues. "How would you do things differently next time?" Dave asked. I spent a lot of time thinking about our early evening badminton games and began to win more consistently. I started to realize that maybe there was something to the sports psychology bogusness after all.

Dave and I started to go running together in a beautiful place called "Garden of the Gods." It's in the northern mountains of Colorado Springs and has canyons of reddish rock. During the runs, he'd explain meditation, centering exercises, and the idea of becoming cognizant of my breath in order to focus attention and bring relaxation to my mind and body. I had yet to understand exactly how I could bring those skills to short track competitions, but I was intrigued enough to try some. We'd spend entire runs practicing relaxation of our bodies, breathing into our legs and fatigued muscles and then trying to push ourselves to new levels. At an elite level, if an athlete can improve execution by even three percent, it makes an enormous difference. Dave's exercises affected my performance.

Dave suggested I start meditating by simply focusing on my breath passively going in and out of my body. If my attention started to drift, I would come back to my breath each time. In the beginning, I drifted a lot. It's really difficult not to think about everything you need to get done: telephone calls, conversations, competitions, skate maintenance, friends, food, etc. Within a few months Dave had me practicing my centering exercises in the bathtub. I like baths so it's a place I'm relaxed anyway, and concentration and distraction control exercises were easier alone, in a calming environment. I didn't focus on how well I wanted to do during competitions or what the other skaters' strengths and weaknesses were. Those early exercises weren't about winning or losing and that made them a valuable tool—something I could build upon in other domains.

In skating, lactic acid buildup, pain, and chronic fatigue are major components, so learning how to relax in the middle of those things is key. Dave taught me how to take the exercises I'd been doing and transfer them to practice, then travel. Finally I used them in the heat box (where skaters wait for their event and everyone is watching each other, the races, and who is moving up to the semis or finals), and on the ice. Every single skill Dave taught me came into play during the 1998-1999 World Cup season.

For the first three World Cup events of the season, I didn't skate much. As the alternate, my opportunities to compete were limited and I had yet to skate well enough to make the top five in the world. But in October, at an exhibition event at a World Cup in Saratoga Springs, I showed such great potential that I earned the chance to race in the individual events at the following World Cup in Szekesfehervar, Hungary. It was one of the best experiences of my career.

Everyone was there—Olympic gold medalist Kim Dong-Sung of Korea and Fabio Carta of Italy (the two fastest short trackers in the world at the time), and four-time World Champion Marc Gagnon of Canada. The atmosphere in the arena was charged. Pat Wentland says I skated like I was "on fire." All I know is that I have never been hungrier, and I wasn't the weakest wolf in the pack anymore.

In the semifinals of the 1500-meters I had to beat Marc Gagnon and come in second to Dong-Sung in order to qualify for the finals. I played it smart and fairly safe and did what I needed to do to get to the finals, finishing third overall for the event. Then on to the 1000-

meters, my best race of the competition. The lineup for the 1000- was overwhelming. I glanced at Dong-Sung, who had just won a gold medal in the Olympics I'd failed to attend, and at Fabio Carta, who was skating incredibly fast. *Please let me do well,* I prayed.

When we shot off from the starting line, I was in fourth place. With four laps to go, I knew that I either had to make a move or I'd lose. But where? There was a tiny gap between Carta and Dong-Sung. I blasted through it and found myself in second place, behind Carta. I was skating out of my mind, everything became automatic and I was flowing, in the zone. I tried to pass Carta on the inside, but I didn't have enough speed. In the final corner I tried again and succeeded. Seconds later I'd won the race. My first World Cup win ever, and one of the first for the United States.

I finished fourth in the 3000-meter race and Dong-Sung set a new world record, which proved to me I'd beaten him while he was skating unbelievably well. I didn't advance past the preliminary heats in the 500-meter race, and in the 5000-meter relay we were poised to take gold but had a fall that put us in sixth place. Overall I placed third for the competition and felt like I was where I should be. Maybe I should have been there in 1997, but I'd come into my own a little bit later than expected.

I left Hungary exhilarated. I was the youngest skater to ever win the 1000-meters at a World Cup. It was a breakthrough moment for me. I'd beaten Carta and Dong-Sung, the fastest skaters in the world. I'd proven to myself that even though I hadn't made the 1998 Olympic team, I belonged with the best skaters in short track. I could compete.

Dave continued to push me all through the fall. I practiced self-talk, positive affirmations, meditation techniques (in the bathtub), and visualization. I worked to maintain a positive attitude about my skating, the sport, and my teammates. The short track team was lucky enough to have Dave travel with us to the Junior World Championships in Montreal, Canada. At 7 P.M., the day before my first race, Dave took me into the empty arena. We went high into the stands and Dave made some suggestions before leaving me alone. I did a centering exercise, concentrating on calming my body and getting into a zone of optimal arousal. Then I worked on getting a race strategy in my head and figuring out exactly what moves I wanted to execute. Finally I put a vivid picture in my mind of what was going to happen during each race.

A day of short track competitions is an extremely up and down experience. There are eight races a day, and you can fall in one and then have to skate again in an hour and put that fall, no matter how spectacular or excruciating, out of your mind. Anything can happen from moment to moment, so having some sort of calming practice and a detailed plan to rely upon is extremely helpful.

"What do *you* want to happen today?" Dave asked when he rejoined me in the stands. He suggested that I imagine potential problems and distractions that could come up and discuss how I was going to handle each one. After we finished, we reflected on some of my goals. It was the first time I'd ever totally mentally prepared and the experience was life changing. I breathed in strength and exhaled relaxation and my final piece of imagery was seeing myself as a cat getting ready to pounce on his prey.

In my mind I was still only halfway up the mountain when I came to compete at the Junior World Championships. I believed I'd fallen off my career path at the Nagano Olympic Trials, and the Worlds events were my chance to start the long climb back up. Dave was with me the whole way as a role model and mentor. Throughout the championships, I'd approach him between races. "How'd I look on the ice?" I'd ask.

"How'd you feel?" Dave replied each time, always deflecting my questions back to me.

During the championships the Koreans played some weird games. The coaches stood on the sidelines yelling instructions to their skaters while someone else blew whistles whenever a skater was about to pass a Korean athlete. When the whistle blew, the Koreans would instantly change tracks to block a pass *before* it was actually made. Every time I'd try to pass one of them, I'd hear the whistle, see them change their tracks, and be forced to bide my time for another opportunity.

What they were doing wasn't illegal—coaches can yell or do anything from the sidelines—but there appeared to be a lot of team skating. Team skating means that together skaters from one country help a team member to win a race. It's frustrating, hard to prove, and very illegal. But I kept my focus, relaxed, and visualized each of my races. The entire competition came down to the 1500-meter finals. If I didn't win that event, I wouldn't get the overall title. I couldn't skate up the inside of the pack because of what the Koreans were doing, so I had to move to the outside to make each pass. An inside pass is easiest, because it's a slingshot move requiring more technique but less power. On the outside, you have to be going much faster because there's a greater distance to span over the top—it's the "big dog."

For the 1500- final, my moves needed to be explosive, or I wouldn't be able to get by the Koreans. In the last lap of the race I passed on the outside and pulled away from the other skaters. When I crossed the finish line my visualizations became a reality. I won the overall event. More importantly, I proved to the short track community that I was back, and I was a serious upcoming contender. I was also the youngest skater to ever win the Junior World title.

In addition to all of the techniques that Dave taught me, something else changed for me at the Worlds. I had always thought that I needed to hang out with other skaters, just to learn something from them. I believed that I could never isolate myself at competitions because I needed to pick up technical tips, learn how to fix my blades, or understand the top competitor's strategy and style. No one ever taught me those things, I picked them up by observing, listening, and asking questions. At Worlds, I finally understood that I was ready to be in my own zone at competitions. Dave had laid the foundations for my mental training and I retreated to a place within myself during and after races where I was quiet, calm, and focused.

Total trust and respect. That's what I felt about Dave after the championship. From that competition forward I never again doubted his knowledge and advice and we became great friends. Several other skaters on the team also started to work more closely with Dave after seeing how much he'd helped me. He had gained their respect too.

After the World Championship, I did several interviews about the event. "I felt strong, mentally and physically, and I was just going for number one," I told reporters. I was articulating my thoughts and direction in a way I'd never done before. I was certain that 1999 was going to be my breakout season.

The difference between the World Championship and World Team Championship is that in the World Team Championship, everyone on the team gets to compete once for each distance. Whoever does best in their bracket (group) during the heats, quarter, and semifinals gets to skate in the finals. I easily made it onto the World Team as one of the top two skaters. The team traveled to the World Team Championship in St. Louis, Missouri.

It was a stressful time. Rumors had been circulating for months that head coach Pat Wentland was going to be let go by the speed skating federation. Pat was a great coach, we were reaching the peak of the season, and any changes could only hurt individual skaters and the team.

But some of the skaters didn't like his coaching anymore. The politics didn't take into account the team's needs.

Despite the stress, I skated well during the championships, won the 1000-meters, and the United States was winning the entire competition. I went into the 500-meter finals full of confidence, and started to chase down Francois Tremblay of Canada, my biggest competition in the 500-meters at the Junior Worlds. He's a strong sprinter but I caught up to him, and was about to make a move when my blade hit one of the blocks. I knew I was in trouble because I went down so fast.

I instantly hurtled toward the wall of the rink and hit incredibly hard. I had trouble breathing from the impact—the wind was knocked out of me. "Keep going, keep going," Pat Wentland called from the sidelines. "You need to finish the race to get your points." There are points for each place and each race and if I didn't complete the 500-meters it would hurt my chances and my team's for medals. I got up and crossed the finish line, but my chest really hurt and something was wrong with my mid- and upper back. When I got off the ice, the trainers checked me over and decided that I had bruised bones in my back. Pat took me out of the rest of the competition and I felt bad because my team had lost its momentum and in the end didn't finish that strongly.

I didn't realize until over a year later that striking the pads had started what was to become a chronic and eventually debilitating back injury. It wasn't until the summer of 2001 that I finally got appropriate care for my back from Dr. Scott Rosenquist, a chiropractor with a master's degree in biomechanics and trauma at Alliance Health Partners Optima Rehabilitation Center in Colorado Springs. By then it was almost too late for me to salvage a chance to compete in the 2002 Olympics—my back was that far gone.

It's important to point out that I could have been more vocal about my injury at the World Team competition. I honestly didn't know how to gauge pain anymore. It was something I lived with as a short track skater—something all athletes are taught to ignore—and I was too young and inexperienced to understand that my back needed more attention than a bag of ice and a massage.

Dislocation-Reorientation-Celebration

"If you don't want to watch skaters crash into the wall, don't come watch short track."

That's what one of the U.S. coaches said during the 2002 Olympics in Salt Lake City. It's that kind of grossly negligent attitude about the safety of skaters that can lead to disaster. We're expected to take risks and as an athlete I accept that, but technology and training allow us to skate faster and harder than we could in the past. Attitudes and safety precautions haven't kept pace. In the United States, both are outdated.

Safety is a huge issue for speed skaters. Even though we wear helmets and cut-proof protection around our necks, the biggest danger is hitting the walls. Currently, the organizers of competitions have the responsibility to make sure that their arenas have *appropriate* pads on the rink walls. That takes money, and most won't spend it unless they're forced to, and they're not.

Right now the pads on the walls of most U.S. arenas are bolted to the border of the rink, which means that when skaters fly into the sides of the ice, they hit a stationary pad held in place by wood or metal and backed by the same. We travel at speeds of up to forty miles per hour so hitting the wall feels like being taken out by a linebacker, except we're wearing a skintight Lycra suit and no shoulder, back, knee, or leg guards.

While spectators love to see crashes, it's important to understand that skaters and their families suffer the consequences. I have a lot of friends who have seriously hurt their backs and necks because of impact. I'm not talking bruises, I'm talking about permanent damage that takes them out of the sport and affects their lives.

In Calgary, Canada, there is a new system for wall pads—they move with the skater upon collision. Tests have shown that they reduce impact by fifty percent. No one can change the pads in the United States except the organizers, and they won't unless the speed skating federation mandates that skaters won't skate until precautions are taken to ensure their safety. Organizers need to be held accountable. At the 2002 Salt Lake City Trials and the Olympic Games, several female skaters were injured. There was a lot more blood than there had to be. The new padding system wasn't used for the rinks in either of the two venues.

But a skater's safety isn't just about the pads on the walls, protective clothing, and the condition of their blades. There's a personal and professional responsibility not to put other skaters in jeopardy. No win is worth hurting someone else. There's the responsibility of each coach to make sure their athletes are physically prepared for races. And the skating federation is answerable for providing well-trained expert coaches on whom skaters can depend.

Pat Wentland was let go as head coach of the U.S. National Team. Susan Ellis replaced him. Susan had coached a few good Canadian skaters, but to my mind she wasn't ready for the responsibility of the National Team. The team flew off to Sofia, Bulgaria, for the World Short Track Speed Skating Championships. I won a silver medal in the 500-meter final, beating Fabio Carta and Eric Bedard, a strong Canadian sprinter. But my back was still aching, and in the end, I took a fourth overall. I tried to apply some of the things Dave had said about taking the positive out of every experience and building from that point. Nothing, he'd told me, is a win or lose situation if you do that. It was a challenging exercise in Bulgaria.

I took a break in August, went up to Seattle and rode my bike and did dry-land workouts with my dad at the high school track. Three workouts a day was the new level of training I implemented while home. I'd heard elite athletes over the years say that they took very little time off between one season and the next, pushing through the pain and their body's exhaustion until they'd struggled off a plateau and reached a new high. I believed I could be one of those athletes. Looking back, I was blinded by my desire and ambition and ignored my persistent health problems to my own detriment.

The fall of 1999 started off at whirlwind speed. I competed in the first World Cup of the season, in Montreal, Canada. Even though I was disqualified in the 500-meters, I came in third in the 1000-meter finals and fifth overall. A week later I raced another World Cup event in Salt Lake City and was second overall. Immediately I returned to Colorado Springs and continued my three workouts a day. I started to catch every little cold anybody had—you name it, I got it.

In December I attended a World Cup in Changchun, China. It was phenomenal. The rink in Changchun is the biggest in the world and short track is one of their most popular sports. There were twelve thousand spectators watching the World Cup event. I'd never skated in front of that kind of crowd. In the United States short track skaters get excited if there are five hundred spectators. China was my first experience with the electricity of screaming fans and how it pushes skaters to a higher level of performance.

I placed first overall and won my first World Cup title as the youngest skater in the sport's history. When I won, I became a household name in China, because rarely in that country does anyone best their national hero, Jiajun Li. I did tons of interviews and was recognized on the street by fans. It was my first brush with fame and at the time it was so positive that I never imagined there could be a downside.

My recurrent illnesses continued. In December 1999, in addition to competitions, skating, traveling, and training, I was still trying to get my high school degree from the Internet Academy. I wanted to graduate with the rest of my class in the spring of 2000, so I pushed myself pretty hard.

I skipped a few smaller competitions but had to fly to Boston in February for the U.S. Championships, a selection event for the U.S. National Team where skaters must make the team so that they can compete in the individual World Cups. The scoring system allotted heavy points for a nine-lap and four-lap time trial and added those to the total points awarded for each place in the finals. I came in second in the nine-lap and won the four-lap. In the finals of the 1500-meters I came in first, which was fortuitous because I fell in the 1000-meters and hit the wall with so much force that I dislocated both my kneecaps. My boots were getting old, starting to crack, and they just didn't support my ankles.

Dislocating your kneecap is extremely painful—it feels razor-sharp, hot like lightning, and the stabs of agony race up your leg and squeeze the breath out of your lungs. I put one kneecap back into place while still on the ice, so that I could stand up. My father and I spent the rest of the day on a very (very) long drive to a Boston emergency room, hours of waiting, x-rays, poking and prodding before I was medically cleared. Needless to say, I was out of the rest of the competition. Luckily, my earlier points had put me in second place overall for the championship. I would still compete in all the individual World Cup events.

Three days later were the Goodwill Games in Lake Placid, New York. I left Boston a day earlier than the rest of the U.S. team and spent my first day in Lake Placid icing my knee and trying to recover. Knees don't like to be dislocated and all the tendons were swollen. I spent the second day skating around on the ice alone, because the team's van didn't leave as planned. I forced myself to train in the silent arena. The third day I received a new pair of boots and tried to break them in. I had to get the rocker right, work on the bend and try to feel good on the ice. New boots are like new shoes, uncomfortable at first. The difference is that if the skates are set up wrong, you don't just get a blister, you fall and potentially slice other skaters or yourself with your blades or hit the wall. On the fourth day, with a sore knee, aching feet, and the feeling that my skates weren't perfect, I tried to compete. The results were disastrous and I fell again in the 1000-meters.

I had a tough time finishing out the winter of 2000. I did well at the World Team Championship in the Netherlands, finishing second in the 3000-meter final against Dong-Sung (only three-hundredths of a second behind the Nagano gold medalist) and beating Carta, Li, and Gagnon. But I was having more and more difficulty recovering from each race.

The lowest point of that season was in March, when I traveled to Sheffield, England for the World Championships. My dad came with me because I'd never been that sick for a competition. I had a 102-degree fever and couldn't stop violently coughing. It took hours for me to fall asleep at night and Dad said that I'd cough until about 4 A.M. Previous tests showed that my red-blood-cell counts were way below normal and my white-cell count was high. I had iron deficiencies and my immune system was no longer functioning.

My dad went to every health store in Sheffield, trying to buy homeopathic remedies, but I was afraid to take them. Athletes are always tested for enhancement performance drugs (doping), and sometimes homeopathic medicines don't show every ingredient. I couldn't take the chance. It was so frustrating to be that sick, and difficult for my father to watch and not be able to help. In the end, I took antibiotics, but that just made me feel weak and sloppy. I didn't compete very well—my best finish was a seventh place.

There were a lot of different reasons for my lack of performance. Number one, I hadn't taken care of my health and I was really sick. Number two, Susan Ellis, the new head coach, had a much different style than Pat. She was focused on drills, strength, mass, and lactic capacity. I had always focused on cardio, biking, being lean, and skating fast. For some reason I didn't really question how well Susan's plans would work for me. Over the winter I'd started to change my technique and focus on consistency instead of speed. I did tons of weight training and my legs were really huge—I was pressing about 1500 pounds. I was strong but I was weighing in at 180 instead of my usual 160 pounds, and I felt heavy on the ice. I had the power to pull away from other skaters to the front of the pack, but after each race I was dead and had a hard time recovering.

When I returned to Colorado Springs for summer training, I met with Tony Bellofato and we decided I needed a new plan. I would go back to the intensive cardiovascular workouts, and we agreed that I had to lose twenty pounds. Tony was psyched to help me get back on track and at the same time I focused on getting healthy and ridding myself of the bronchial infection for good. I thought I'd finally realized that no matter how hard I trained, if I was sick and didn't listen to my body and protect it, I wouldn't be able to compete at the elite level and win. However, I still had more lessons to learn.

I was admittedly mad at Susan for most of the summer. She'd put me on a program I felt had messed up my body and now I had to work unbelievably hard to get back on track. When I told her that I was going to do my own training she agreed that it was probably a good idea. I was unhappy with her training methods, but I admit that when I saw my body changing, and I gained weight and lost endurance, I should have said, "No more."

During the summer I pretty much trained by myself because the other skaters had gone home for a break. Even if I'd wanted to go home, in Seattle I couldn't get the ice time I needed. It wasn't readily available and it was still too expensive for Dad and me. I'd learned over time that at home I would quickly lose the "feel" of the ice, no matter how much I trained on land, and would start off the season behind the curve.

I spent hours on the StairMaster that summer, just dripping sweat. I'd bike in the mountains at high altitude for hours a day, then go for runs four times a week with Pat Wentland and his wife. Pat wasn't coaching at the time, but he lived in Colorado Springs and was willing to help me work out. Since he was the coach who had fought to get me onto the Junior Development Program and helped make me the number one short tracker in the world within a year of my initial training, I trusted Pat to help me get back in shape. Together we looked for the steepest hills, hardest climbs, and most difficult rides. Within a month my body fat percentage dropped by 6 percent. I felt light and my vertical jump (overall body strength) was getting higher. After the second month I lost another 2 percent body fat and got my weight down to 158 pounds.

I started to work with Steve Gough, the new assistant team coach for the 2000-2001 season. Steve was on the 1994 Canadian Olympic team but had a serious injury that changed the alignment of his leg so he could no longer compete. Steve was not only an amazing skater, he was a fantastic coach. He just has the eye. He can watch me skate and knows what I need to do. He's seen so many videotapes of me that he's a technical expert. I believe he can be one of the best coaches in the world, plus he makes my blades feel good, something I had under-rated in the past but now understood meant the difference between winning, losing, or getting seriously hurt.

I told Steve I wanted to be the best skater on the team.

"All right, cool," Steve replied in his usual, laid-back manner.

We started to do extra workouts, and this time, I wasn't stepping up my training when I was already physically drained. I felt strong enough to put in the extra effort. I'd sprint on the bike with very little resting time (fifteen seconds between sprints), and do an hour every day of dry-land jump workouts—jumping with my body at a ninety-degree angle in a crouched skating position. In addition I did my weight program with Tony, skated, and still ran four times a week.

Steve told me that I was going to surprise a lot of people that year. I hoped and dreamed he was right. When my teammate Rusty returned to Colorado Springs to train for the season, I'd follow him on the ice, because he always does such impressive lap times. At first I'd struggle to keep up with him, but felt myself improving every day. I was going faster and faster and I was happy. Not only was my physical training going well, but after three months, my blood work had returned to normal. I was healthy.

Rusty was a really positive force during my life at that time. He's an incredibly good skater and an extremely fast sprinter, but more impor-tantly, he and I have been training partners for years. We have a strong friendship and mutual respect for each other. He's from California, so we just have that West Coast connection. In practice Rusty and I pull each other along, no matter how tough the day. In competitions, we're fierce adversaries who are still happy for each other's victories. A bit older than me, Rusty has always shown by example how to carry your-self at the highest standards of short track, competition, and sports-manship.

❋ ❋ ❋

I started dominating the sport by the fall of 2000. But there were factors at play, other than my abilities, which were conspiring to take one of the best coaches I've ever had away from the senior team. For months I had not been working much with the head coach. In fact, when Susan tried to get me on the same program as the skaters who'd returned for training, I'd refused. I was finally standing up for what I knew I needed to do to be the best skater possible. I was one of the top three skaters in the world and I had to work with someone whose experience could help guide my career. Steve was a world-class athlete, a technical genius, and incredibly valuable to his skaters. His training worked well with my style and I trusted him. Unfortunately, Steve had not been working closely with his boss. Susan started to complain about him to the federation. I felt the tension between my coaches, but tried to stay out of the politics.

The first World Cup of the 2000-2001 season was held on October 21 in Calgary, Canada. The instant I got on the ice, I felt great. Each surface in every arena is different, depending on the temperature, the rink, and myriad other factors down to the water used to make the ice. In Calgary, the ice was perfect for my style of skating, which is aggressive, really aggressive, around the corners. When the ice isn't good my blade slips and I lose a lot of speed. In Calgary I could go fast and I was ready to send a message to the world of short track: _Look at me._

The top guys were there: Dong-Sung, one of the most dominant skaters in short track with flawless technical abilities and the best in the world as far as physical capabilities, and Li from China, who is called the "Old Mayan" or "Mr. Consistent" and who rarely if ever makes mistakes. He is, if not the fastest guy out there, the one who always has the most heart. Everyone was skating tough, including Marc Gagnon and Rusty. I practiced the techniques Dave had taught me both before and during each race. I visualized myself at the starting line, a powerful cat springing forward and tearing across the ice. I planned to attack and win.

I took off explosively in the 1500-meters of the Calgary World Cup, but let the other skaters chase me and catch me on purpose. *Relax, relax, relax,* I told myself. Gagnon whizzed by and I sat on his tail, drafting a little bit. The last two laps he started skating harder, pushing me to keep up with him. I looked back and saw Dong-Sung fighting to come up to the front. The gap between us was widening and I set my sights on Gagnon. I turned into the last lap and burst ahead, easily winning the race. Everyone was stunned by how much spring I had left in my legs at the end.

Gagnon, a fierce competitor, came up and congratulated me with a pat on the back and a big smile. I really respect him as a skater and a person. He has a lot of integrity and that's something I try to emulate. Later, my own style of congratulating my competitors would become a controversy, even though most skaters, even the serious Koreans, are known for occasional smiles and backslaps.

Everything just fell into place at that World Cup. I won the title at every distance—500-, 1000-, and 1500-meters. I set an American record en route to winning the men's 1500-meters and another American record in the men's 500-meters. I was disqualified in the 3000-meters for cross-tracking, but everyone there knew it was a bad call. Dong-Sung came up to me after the race and said in his best English, "You're number one, you're the best." I was so psyched that he felt that way because he's such an incredible athlete. I wish that today I could skate as well as I skated in Calgary. I was really light and strong and the up and down motion of skating was so repetitive and comfortable that it was a motion without thought of pain.

I continued to dominate at the next World Cup event in Provo, Utah. Overall I came in second, but I couldn't really do anything wrong on the ice. Everything I'd been working for was happening. I won the 500-meters, beating both Li from China and the gold medalist at Nagano, Nishitani from Japan. My start was explosive, which was a good sign that I was skating well across the board. Some skaters are great at the 3000-meters or the 1000-, but can't win a 500-meter race. I was trying to do well at each event, which requires different skills—strength, endurance, power, and patience. Provo was also the first time I realized how much the media was focused on short track as an emergent sport for the Games, and on me in particular. There was a press conference and most of the questions were aimed at me . . . in a good way. I loved the positive attention, but I had yet to learn about the dark side of the media.

I spent December in Tokyo at one of the Asian World Cup and won the gold in the 1500-meters. I missed the 500- finals because my blade clipped against a Canadian skater's and I lost my edge. I went to the World Cup in China and for the second straight year I won the overall title. I loved skating in front of thousands of fans, and I think it helped prepare me for the 2002 Olympics—nothing could compare to the spotlight, the jam-packed arena at the Salt Lake City Games and the deafening cheers. At the end of the Asian World Cup, when the Korean and Chinese coaches were asked who the best skater in the world was, they said, "Apolo Ohno."

Merry Christmas . . . I was the only skater left at the training center for Christmas of 2000. All the other skaters went home. But since I wouldn't be able to get on the ice in Seattle, my dad came down for the holiday to help me train, and we made it a great Christmas together.

Every morning we went into the rink, rolled up our sleeves and hung the pads on the walls. Usually the entire team (sixteen people) works together to hang the heavy, bulky pads. Dad just poured sweat and we got the job done, wrestling every square onto the wall and then moving on to the next so that when I finished weight training and skated onto the ice, the rink was ready.

My dad spent hours filming my skating and timing my laps. After practice I'd watch the videos and then go to the bleachers at Colorado College so I could run up and down the steep stairs. Dad kept me company, patiently waiting, bundled against the cold.

We worked together as partners that holiday. I'd pushed past the difficult days of puberty and the teenage inclination to shove a parent away, ignoring the tangle of tugging emotional strings. My father remembers thinking that Christmas that he finally had his son back. I just remember being grateful that my dad was there.

❄

Apolo Anton Ohno at ages three
(with balloons) and four

❄

Apolo, age four, visits Santa.

———

*An energetic five-year-old Apolo
rides his bike.*

A weekend spent outdoors for eight-year-old Apolo

———

At just eight years old, Apolo took the gold medal at the 1990 Northwest Regional Championships in quad skating.

✺

Trying a different set of wheels at age eight

———

Eight-year-old Apolo stands proudly with his Mid-America Speed League trophy.

❄

Clowning around with his father, Yuki

———

Team Ohno preparing for a meet

✳

Apolo, age twelve, at the U.S.
Championships

❄

Apolo wins the gold medal at the 2002 Salt Lake City Olympic Winter Games.

❄

At a 2002 post-Oscar party, with
Harrison Ford (top) and Ozzy and
Sharon Osbourne (bottom)

Climbing the Mountain

I finished establishing my short track résumé in Austria at the February 2001 World Cup event. If there were any doubters about my abilities before Austria, they couldn't question who I was, what I'd done, or where I was going after that World Cup. I won the 1500-meter, 500-meter, and 3000-meter finals. That meant I could sprint, compete at mid-distances, and be a powerful presence in the endurance races. I was awarded the overall World Cup title for each distance and for the entire year. I felt like I was soaring; that nothing could stop me. I was finally at the top of the mountain, but I had forgotten how slippery the slope could be.

I flew with the U.S. team to Japan in March 2001 for the World Team Championships, held one weekend before the World Championships in Korea. I initially had a blade problem during practice, and called my dad in Seattle at 4 A.M. for suggestions. Steve hadn't made the trip with the team (the federation was already plotting to replace him) and Susan had no idea how to fix my skates. I ended up having to endure a bad bend and partially stripped edges because there was no time to find an appropriate technician before the event—partly my fault because I should always be prepared.

Three days before the competition I went to a Wednesday weight session at the Japanese facility. It's typical to do very light weight training during the days between competitions. I went into the gym feeling strong. My personal training schedule was right on track. I was definitely thinking about summer 2001, my goals, and the workouts needed to make it into the 2002 Olympics. Right in the middle of a weight repetition, I felt something go very wrong in my back. It wasn't a tear or a pop; it was a deep pain that felt like it was in my vertebrae. It literally took my breath away.

The trainers weren't certain what I'd done—they're not doctors. They suggested I ice, get deep tissue massage, and take it easy until the competition on Saturday. I had trouble standing up straight and when I bent over, getting upright required me to use my abdominal muscles much more than I did normally.

I raced as scheduled on Saturday. My back was aching, but something was also wrong with my calves and ankles. They felt weak, which I later learned was a result of the muscles I'd torn and a bulging disk that shot pain down through my leg. Halfway through the competition my back started to go into spasms, and I could barely get into the correct aerodynamic position to skate. I considered telling Susan Ellis to pull me out, but the team needed me and I went onto the ice and won the 3000-meters with all of my energy.

The U.S. relay team also needed to win a semifinal in order to make the finals. If we lost, we'd have to race again, against additional teams, for a last-ditch chance to still make the finals. When one of the U.S. skaters fell during the semis, we were forced into another full-out competition.

The back spasms got worse—they were agonizing—but it's extremely rare for me to ever ask to be taken out of a race. Still, I did let Susan know I was in pain.

Susan explained that I was the strongest the team had. She wanted to put me in, and I went out there to do the second race for her and the team. I came in second to last because I was so dead. As it turns out, both my evaluation and concerns were unfortunately very valid.

✲ ✲ ✲

No time to see a doctor, no time spent to recover. We flew directly to the World Championships in Korea. I was nervous because these were the first senior Worlds that I had a chance to win. It was the biggest competition of the year, and I really wanted to succeed. I mentally shelved my back pain, which seems impossible, but I'd spent my life learning how to accomplish that kind of focus. Being elite-level athletes, we shun pain and try to accept it as an everyday kind of thing— it's what separates us from regular athletes, and both elevates our performances and tears our bodies apart.

My first final, the 1500-meters, I was in the perfect position to win with three laps to go . . . and then I hesitated for half a lap. It totally killed me because Gagnon came on the outside and Li came up on the inside and they gapped me, putting me in third. There was enough space that I couldn't draft off them and had to fight my way back up to the front of the pack. In the last half lap I made a nice move on Li, but he defended his line with his elbow. I lost my balance because the move, which is illegal but not uncommon, caught me so off guard. I ended up finishing in fourth place just because I hesitated.

I can't blame the race on my back. I think that I was just worked after a season of dominating short track. I was one of the few guys who'd been to five World Cup events that year, and I was tired. I bombed the 500-meters. In the 1000- semis, I came back and won after the Koreans spent the race trying to tire me out with one guy leading in the beginning while the next sat behind me drafting.

The Koreans were team skating once again, but I was pumped going into the 1000-meter finals because I'd still beaten them. My biggest competition was Li of China. I was in the lead with two laps to go and again I hesitated. Li passed me on the inside and totally took off. He's such a dominant, consistent skater—he's pretty much got the whole package plus mad experience. I tried to get by him in the final lap, but ended up second. I was bummed because if I'd won that race, there was a chance I could have won the overall championship.

I still had the chance to win second overall at the Worlds and I was determined to fight for that place. It came down to the 3000-meters. I was in the lead, but with three laps to go I hesitated yet again, which allowed Gagnon to get right on my tail. He couldn't afford to let me win the race because that would put him into third overall for the event, with me in second. If he beat me and Li, he would win overall. That would be his fifth World Championship gold. But I managed to hold Gagnon off and won the 3000-meters. I received the overall silver for the championship. It felt good because I'd proven I was consistent at the Worlds, even despite an injury, and consistency is the number-one goal, especially going into an Olympic year.

By the end of the 2000-2001 season I claimed twelve victories on the World Cup circuit—four in the 1500-, one in the 1000-, three in the 500-, and four in the 3000-meters. However when I returned to Colorado for spring training, my back was raw. I didn't go into rehab like I should have. Later that summer, the team traveled to Salt Lake City for a training camp. The skaters had the opportunity to try out different equipment, including manufacturers' newest boots and blades.

I had frequently used a weight vest to strengthen my back and legs, but at the camp I couldn't finish more than twenty laps even without the vest. *What's wrong with me? I can usually do sixty laps with a vest.* I pushed myself, making sixty laps my goal, then eighty laps with the weight vest. The pain in my back got worse and worse. I disregarded it, thinking my back was just weak.

I returned to Colorado Springs to continue training, once again ignoring all the health warnings and lessons I should have learned. It seems crazy when I look back, but I was overwhelmed by a desire to reach a higher level of fitness. At nineteen I still believed I was in total control of my body and should be invincible. During that time, I'd skate the men's practice back-to-back with the women's team practice, plus do dry-land workouts, weights, biking, and running. By May, I couldn't even make it through a single practice. Severe muscle spasms forced me off the ice. Panicked, I saw my Olympic dreams sliding away from me.

My back injury probably began after my fall in 1999. But everyone takes a beating in short track, and I didn't focus for long on any discomfort because it was normal. But by the end of May 2001, the pain was no longer normal. I finally went to see Dr. Scott Rosenquist. Scott is a chiropractor who practices at the Colorado Springs Alliance Health Partners Optima Rehabilitation Center. He was extremely generous with his time and energy through the course of my rehabilitation and I'm very grateful to him.

Scott took x-rays and I had an MRI. He diagnosed facet syndrome in my lower back. The muscles were so tight that they would spasm every time I'd bend over and try to skate. In addition, I had a psoaz and quadratis lumboram tear, and the facet and the psoaz muscle were so contracted that they were causing my L-5, S-1 lower-back disk to bulge, resulting in severe leg pain. My legs were remarkably strong, despite the bulge, but my lower back was very weak, and my multifidi tissue was producing marked pain.

Scott said I'd need eight weeks of intensive work before I even thought about getting back on the ice. It would probably take three months before I was 80 percent recovered. He suggested rehabilitation exercises, myofacial release, and deep tissue work to loosen up the muscles, which were locked and had hardened to protect the injured areas of my back. He also warned that although he thought he could help me, if there were any signs he might be hurting me, he would stop the treatment. My coaches and trainers supervised the rehabilitation but Scott quickly inspired all of our trust.

The facts were still daunting: months of rehabilitation with no guarantee that I'd get better without surgery, or that I'd be able to start training in time for the Olympic Games. I couldn't skate; I couldn't stand upright; it was seven months before the Olympic Trials. I tried not to appear weak to other skaters, but there were times when I'd bend over and couldn't stand back up. I felt like an old man and watched as the years of hard work and training disappeared from my muscles, leaving me weak and out of shape. All I could do was continue with the rehab and light exercise and just pray that I'd heal.

In early August, after three months of physical therapy, my dad came to visit me. He knew that I was depressed so we drove to Steamboat Springs, a mountain resort in Colorado, and spent the weekend outdoors. I felt like a little kid again. We climbed up as many of the hills and mountains as we could. Even though it was late in the summer, there was still a lot of snow at the higher elevations. We were post-holing (sinking in up to our knees) and getting soaked, but it felt great. I experienced some pain, but it wasn't too bad and the altitude didn't bother me at all. Plus, there's something so healing about just being outside. I was spending too much time in my dark little dorm room, brooding over my injury and the future.

We hiked for three days. It wasn't what the doctor or physical therapist had ordered and I wouldn't suggest anyone with a bulging disk try it as a remedy. But I felt like I was finally on the mend, and despite the odds, my back was healing in record time. It would be a tough road back to top condition, but at least I would have the chance to travel down it and give 110 percent.

The U.S. Speedskating federation replaced Steve Gough in the summer of 2001. Susan had reported that he was not working well with her or for the team. Steve was a guy who would get up at 4 A.M. to work on skaters' blades. He was a brilliant technical coach and he gave his all to every skater. When his job was threatened very few skaters stepped up to try and protect him. I wrote a letter to the federation in support of Steve and was disappointed to find I was the only skater trying to help. It wasn't a great move for my career since Susan was still the head coach, but it had to be done. Steve attempted to keep his job, agreeing to change his style and methods of communication for another chance, but it was too late.

My training for the Olympic Trials started in late August 2001. Steve's absence and the short time frame to the trials stressed me out. I never missed a practice. There were still days when I'd have back spasms and have to leave the ice because the pain was too much to bear. But I wanted to show everyone I was getting strong. Short track is as much a mental game as a physical one and I needed to exhibit a tough exterior or other skaters would believe they could beat me. Believing is one step closer to achieving a goal.

Despite my own efforts to remain low profile through my recovery, rumors within the skating world flew. "Ohno's in bad shape. Apolo's injured. He's out of the running. Ohno will never make it to the Games." Everyone's got a computer, and I could just hear all those clicking fingers on keyboards spreading the news that I wasn't a contender for the 2002 Games. I tried to stay focused and let the whispers pass by without engaging anyone. It wasn't productive to confront other skaters. I had to look inward, find my strength, heal, and then come back more powerful than before. Narrowing in on what I could do well, I focused on dry-land workouts and biking. I became an animal on the land. I was only 70 percent rehabilitated but I hoped that the next 30 percent would come on the way to the trials.

Scott did not believe my back was ready in the fall of 2001 for the stress and pressure of travel and the first World Cup events in Korea and China. Disappointed, I withdrew from the competitions. My coach was not happy with me, but I finally knew that if I wasn't vocal and didn't stick up for myself and my needs, no one would. I wasn't going to risk going into the Olympic Trials with any more injuries than I already had.

In a sad turn of events, the terrorist actions of September 11 occurred. The U.S. team cancelled their trip to the fall World Cup competitions. Everyone on the team was devastated by the attack in New York. I remember that we tried to attend practice that day, but no one could perform and we eventually went back to the dorm to watch the television coverage in huddled silence. While I did not lose any family or close friends in the attack, my heart goes out to everyone who did and to the people who lost their lives. I added my voice to all of theirs, asking "Why?"

By the Calgary World Cup in October 2001, I simply had to start competing. The Olympic Trials were in December—I needed to prove to myself, as well as the world community of skaters, that I was back. I wasn't sure if I'd be successful. I still had 15 percent of my rehabilitation left, and in Calgary I had trouble with my blades, which I could not completely fix.

I was disqualified in Calgary during the finals of the 1500-meters and I started to lose confidence. Still, I found a chance to pass Dong-Sung in the 1000-meters and took first, following it with a second in the 3000-meters. Both were important mental wins. I wasn't at peak performance, but I was once again in the game. That is, until the 5000-meter relay.

The team was doing a time trial—trying to set a new U.S. record for the 5000-meters. I came around the corner and just broke out, the ice giving way beneath my blade. I lost my edge and hurtled headfirst into the wall. My helmet flew off from the impact. I tried to stand but was too stunned. I fell, got back up, and fell back down again. I'd rung my bell and suffered a concussion. Everyone thought I was really hurt, but I finally got off the ice. I was done for the day. It was a far cry from the year before, but I was undaunted and determined to continue and make yet another successful comeback.

The World Qualifiers are a pre-Olympic event that decides which countries can attend the Games and how many skaters each can bring. Each team has to do well, because only the top countries get to compete in short track in the Olympics (otherwise, the Games would be neverending). If the U.S. didn't qualify, there wouldn't be an Olympic Trials for the Games, because none of us would be going. Qualifiers are obviously one of the most important events of the season. I won the 1500-meters by a huge gap. While I was eliminated in the semifinals of the 500-, the team had performed well enough to attend the Games and to bring the maximum number of skaters (five plus an alternate). Individually, I had earned a chance to compete at the Olympic Trials.

I wasn't thrilled with my performance at the qualifiers. My back recovery had started to plateau, but it was still 15 percent away from full recovery. I was extremely frustrated. A close family friend recommended Dr. Lavine, an osteopathic physician. Osteopathy is a full-fledged medical discipline based primarily on the manual diagnosis of impaired function resulting from loss of movement of all kinds of tissue. It's an art, science, and technique. An art, because people who practice it have to understand how to approach a patient to stimulate and restore health; a science because it's based on physiology and anatomy; and a technique because osteopathy uses only manual procedures. I flew to Tacoma, Washington, to see Dr. Lavine. The visit was so gentle and easy, that I wasn't sure how to evaluate my treatment. I'd never seen that kind of doctor before, but the results, combined with my continued rehabilitation in Colorado with Scott, made me a believer. Dr. Lavine would end up flying to Salt Lake City during the Olympic Games to treat me for the flu and the gash on my leg. Just like Scott Rosenquist, he's part of my team, incredibly learned and generous.

※ ※ ※

I truly didn't know if my back was going to be completely healed by the time of the Olympic Trials, let alone the Games. My volume of training was enormous and intense, but a lot of it was biking and dry-land and I was still plagued by muscle spasms on the ice if I pushed too hard. I had to work out alone much of the time, because all of my training partners needed to keep a different schedule. Still, I trained six days a week, sometimes seven, and my back had to recover despite the grueling schedule I kept. I was no longer blind to the injury, but if I didn't train hard, my rehabilitation wouldn't matter because I would-n't make it to the Olympics. Time had quite simply run out.

In addition to dealing with my back and training, the media hype for the Olympic Games had begun. My agents at IMG (International Management Group), Janey Miller and Heather Novickis, were sched-uling interviews and opportunities with sponsors. These were chances for me to help promote the sport of short track and also to gain finan-cial support for the weighty expense of training as a world-class ath-lete. My father had shouldered the cost of my pursuit alone, without complaint, and I finally had the opportunity to help him out.

My schedule became extremely hectic—*Sports Illustrated,* Nike appearance, shooting a drug-free campaign for the U.S. Olympic Committee, *GQ (Gentlemen's Quarterly)* magazine, and NBC prepar-ing their background films for the Games. If things hadn't felt so crazy, I might have enjoyed all the attention. But I was trying to maintain sanity in an insane environment and something had to give.

Two and a half weeks before the Olympic trials, Shani and I were driving home from practice and the roads were slushy, but not too bad. We were in the outside lane on a divided six-lane road going ten miles under the speed limit, which was forty-five miles per hour. All of a sudden my SUV started to veer to the left. *What the hell is going on?* I wondered. *I'm not trying to turn.* I looked in my rearview mirror, thinking that someone had bumped the car and I just hadn't felt it. No one was there. We kept veering, sliding across three lanes on what we later discovered was a patch of black ice. Seconds later we hit the median. I looked over at Shani. "You okay?" BOOM! We flipped over the median and rolled twice into oncoming traffic. The SUV crumpled like tin foil (total devastation), but there were no oncoming cars and we escaped to safety. It was the scariest moment of my life. I thought I was going to die, and I thought my best friend, Shani, was going to go too.

Speedbump

I didn't know until after the Nagano Olympic Trials how important being in the Games was to me. I was devastated and almost didn't return to short track. Going into the 2002 Olympic Trials in Salt Lake City, I already *knew* how important the Games were, so there was much more pressure to perform. My back still wasn't 100 percent and I'd just had a near-death car accident and a lapse in my recovery. I was afraid that after years of tremendously hard work, both physical and mental, and a total dedication to my sport, my back would give out on me and I wouldn't make it into the Olympics.

I had been training for the past few months with Tony Goskowicz, who had become the assistant coach for the Olympic year. Tony was on the U.S. 1994 Olympic Team, and he was a dominant skater throughout 1995-96. I was on the World Team with him in 1997 and in '98 we skated together on the national team. Tony was my buddy, and throughout the fall he worked out with me. There's a cobbled road that goes up the mountains outside Colorado Springs. It's dirt and extremely steep and every Friday we'd run up it. It was a tough three-hour workout and Tony never made me do it alone. I really respect and look up to Tony's physical abilities. He's strong, can push through the pain like no other, and he helped me train again like I was insane—it felt good. Despite the ups and downs, I started to think I had a chance at the trials.

The Olympic Trials are not just a matter of which skater is the strongest. You've got to get through the time trials, heats, quarters, and semifinals. By the time the finals roll around, you've already raced up to five times so you're tired and your legs are fatigued. Mentally you think the other guys are always stronger, because they will never let themselves look tired. You have to deal with the strategy of who's going to do what in each race, and it takes a lot out of you. You've got three or four other guys out there trying to beat you each race, so you have to beat them, or make them beat you if that's your strategy.

Everybody wants to be up front, and if you're in that position and a better skater is behind you, you don't know if he's resting or really tired or if he's about to make a pass. You can never look back without losing time and risking your position. If you're not in front and you want to pass, you have to go even faster than the skater in front of you to take the inside. An outside pass requires precise setup and even more speed. If a skater sees you before you try to pass, he can pick up his pace and widen the gap. You have to be sneaky and subtle. Passing on the outside is the big dog—it's over the top, takes tons more energy and you can be left hanging if the first skater anticipates the attack. The other danger is losing your position because the guys behind you can slide through the space left open by your movement to the outside.

If I'm strong enough, I will go to the outside every time because it's the cleanest way to pass and it's a sign of strength. It humiliates the other skater because it clearly shows that he's not fast enough. But no matter how good I am, there are so many other variables that affect my performance: the federation and their politics, the referees (nobody can control them and they're not always unbiased), my blades, other skaters cross-tracking, team skating, the media. . . .

It's been said that anything can happen in short track and usually does. Still, I don't think anyone was expecting the controversy that ensued after the U.S. Olympic Trials, least of all, me.

✳ ✳ ✳

I did not want to write about the 2001 Salt Lake City Olympic Trials *at all.*
Nothing, nada, zilch, zero. From the onset of the "controversy," I was silent.
I honestly believed that the truth would come out and the world would real-
ize that the unhappiness of a few people shouldn't taint the Olympic Games.

It was hard to ignore the publicity. Even if I didn't watch television,
read the newspapers or magazine articles, the local Colorado Springs
newspaper is everywhere at the Olympic Training Center. I couldn't
avoid the pictures and headlines. I couldn't get away from the questions from other athletes. All I wanted to do was train for the
Olympics, fulfill a dream, and win a medal for my country. Instead I
was forced to become a player in a tawdry affair that wasn't worthy of
mention in print, let alone any time or mental focus.

In the end the dispute at the Olympic Trials took more away from
the sport than it did from me personally. It put a lot of stress on my
family, especially my dad, and my friends and fellow skaters. It was sad
and ugly, unfortunate and unnecessary.

So why am I writing about it? I've learned that if you ignore a controversy, it doesn't just go away. I have taken the high road, and will
continue to do so. But if I didn't write about this, people would wonder why. In truth, it's probably a lose-lose situation, because people
will always try to find fault with what I say.

You'll notice as you read on that I don't use the name of the person
who filed the grievance. I call him "the cockroach," or in short, "the
roach." He's already gotten too much attention and I don't think he
deserves any more airtime. Totally not worth it. So let's talk about the
"big controversy" at the Olympic Trials, which was me not winning
the 1000-meter finals and the roach's reaction.

The Olympic Trials are different from the World Qualifiers. They're not
about *if* or *how many* U.S. skaters are going to the Games, they're about

who is going from the U.S. National Team, period. My goal at the December 2001 trials was to become one of the top two skaters in every distance so that I'd have the opportunity to compete in all four Olympic events.

I trained right up until the moment I left for Salt Lake City. I'd get up at 6 A.M., skate, ice my back, eat, rest up, and then do several hours of dry-land. The following two hours were spent in the park, running, then resting, eating, and weight training until 5 P.M. After weights I'd hit the sports medicine center for a rubdown, then eat at 7 P.M., work on my blades, and watch videotapes of skating.

There were a lot of strong U.S. team members going into the trials at the Utah Olympic Oval. Shani Davis had been first overall at the 2001 U.S. Junior Short Track Championships and had set the U.S. speed record in the 1000-meters. Rusty Smith was a member of the men's gold medal-winning 5000-meter relay at the 2001 World Short Track Championships and a 1998 Olympian. Ron Biondo hadn't trained with us that summer, but he'd earned a gold medal at the 2001 U.S. Junior Short Track Championships. J.P. Kepka was fourth overall at the 1999 U.S. Junior Short Track Championships and fifth overall at the 2001 U.S. Short Track Championships, and Dan Weinstein was third in the 1000-meters and seventh overall in the final 2001 World Cup standings and had skated at the 1998 Olympics.

Dealing with the distractions and pressure at the trials was the toughest aspect. I tried to mentally prepare for the races by going through the visualization and relaxation routines that Dave had taught me. I purposefully stayed at a different hotel than the rest of the U.S. skaters for the trials so that I wouldn't have to be involved in any politics or the mental b.s.

I'm great friends with some of the skaters on the team. Many of us have traveled together and lived in the same dorm for years. We've grown up with each other and that forms a tight bond. But at Olympic Trials, I don't talk to anyone—I'm very quiet, focused, and in my own zone before a race. Short track is an individual sport, and you can't be friends on the ice. It won't work.

The Olympic Trials are a two-week process. The first Friday is the 1000-meter time trials and the 444-meter trials (the nine and four laps). The format is "pursuit-style." You're paired up with one other skater and start at opposite ends of the short track course. Then you run laps—there are preliminaries, heats, quarter, and semifinals, and then finals. This determines the top sixteen skaters who will go on to compete in the rest of the trials for those events.

On Friday, December 12, I won the 1000-meter time trial. Ron took second and Rusty finished third. I entered my own zone during that trial and don't even remember skating, but I clocked in at 1:24.196, which is unbelievably fast. The second fastest time was 1:26.925. That's a big difference.

My confidence started to soar. I knew that if I could stay focused, I'd do great things. Later that day I won the 500-meter time trial by more than a second with Rusty in second and Ron third. The way the scoring for the Olympic Trials worked, winning both time trials put me in first place with 1,974 points. Ron and Rusty were tied at 987 points.

The 1500-meter final was held on Saturday. Dan Weinstein and I raced each other throughout the final and I knew that at the speed we were going the time would be fast. I came in first at 2:13.728. I had now won the first three events at the trials. I was achieving my goal of coming in the top two in every race. Plus I had 2,691 points. Rusty had earned 1,597 and Ron was in third with 1,021 points. I was over-joyed.

I rested during the week between the first and second set of Olympic trial events, doing only light training and short practices. On Friday, December 21, I won every heat for the 500-meters. I took the final, setting a new U.S. record in the process. J.P Kepka finished second, Rusty took third, and Dan finished fourth. I was on fire. I had now secured my position in the 500- and 1500-meter races at the Olympics. I led the trials with 6,909 points.

The final event for the short track Olympic trials, the 1000-meters, was held on Saturday, December 22. I'd long ago secured enough points to make the team and to skate the individual distances at the Games. Reporters asked me, "Are you going to try to sweep, Apolo?" I told them, "No, I'm going to try to stay healthy and accomplish my goals. That's not one of them."

Nishitani, the skater from Japan who'd won a gold medal in the 500-meters at the Nagano 1998 Olympics was injured at Japan's Olympic Trials one month prior to the 2002 Games. He competed in Salt Lake City with three pins in his ankle. He was no longer the same skater. Injuries happen all the time and there's no guarantee that you will recover. I'd had so many injuries and illnesses and struggled to come back time and again that there was no way I was going to risk my chance to compete at the Games.

For Shani Davis, the 1000-meters was his last chance. "I have to do it. Now or never. Either now, or wait another four years," he told the media. In the semifinals Shani had beaten the roach, who as a result became the skater then sixth overall. That meant the roach ended up in a B final, and his fate was no longer in his own hands. If Shani won the A final, he'd make the team. If he didn't, the roach would. In my opinion the roach lost his place on the Olympic team in the semis, by not beating Shani. In addition, Rusty had to finish in front of Ron in order to qualify to skate the 1000-meters at the Olympics.

Shani started out in front and was leading most of the race. The 1000 is his event. Despite his inconsistent performance during the preliminary heats at the trials, Shani had set the U.S. record only months before. He had confidence that he could pull something off, plus he had absolutely nothing to lose. Rusty sat in second during the finals, drafting and waiting for a chance to pass Shani. He tried a few times, but the ice broke out from under him and he wasn't able to make it. With four laps to go, I was passed by another skater in such a bad pass that I almost went down. I saw my career flash before my eyes and had to remind myself to relax and take it easy.

Rusty looked back and saw that there was some space between him and me, and that Ron was behind me. Ron was his biggest concern, because they were competing for an individual spot. Careers hung on that race and it was time to play it smart. Rusty clung to Shani's lead, unable to pass but not giving up his second-place position or risking a fall. Shani won the final, barely beating Rusty. I placed third and Ron took fourth.

Shani had won the race, though the roach later tried to take away his accomplishment of being the first African American to make the Winter Olympics skating team. I went over to Shani after the race and congratulated him with a smile and hug. It was an extremely natural reaction for me, something I'd done to countless skaters in different races. I was glad Shani had done so well. I felt that I had too, skating safely and protecting my place as a competitor for the Games. Someone made a comment that since I showed such happiness for Shani, it "implied wrongdoing." It blows my mind that it's "implied wrongdoing" to be a good sport.

The Olympic Trials were over in my mind, and with less than a month to go it was time for the short track team to focus on the 2002 Games. But we all know that is not what happened.

A complaint was filed by the roach with U.S. Speedskating on December 27, 2001, alleging that two skaters "conspired to fix" the final of the men's 1000-meter race. It was alleged that Rusty and I "colluded," enabling Shani to qualify for the Olympic team and giving Rusty the 1000-meter berth. The roach's attorney, Kevin Duff, stated: "We believe that the result of the race was predetermined by the conduct of one or more participants in the race, and we've expressed to the USOC that we believe that this is a violation both of the U.S. Speed-skating and the U.S. Olympic Committee code of conduct." The funny thing is that there's no rule in any short track rule book stating that I personally "had to win" that race—a win is based on talent, athleticism, technique, the ice, and other skaters, and there's no way to predetermine all of those things. No way.

When asked about the 1000-meter final, Susan Ellis intimated that I had not tried my best. "The talk and suspicion is kind of troubling. But Shani skated a great race, that's the bottom line," Susan said. She could have said the idea that any of the skaters on the U.S. National Team would conspire to fix a race was ridiculous. Instead she opened a floodgate of media speculation and failed to even mention that Shani owned the 1000-meter record.

Some people think that Susan was using me as a pawn to keep Shani off the Olympic team. I don't know if that's true, because he's such a fantastic athlete and competitor that any short track coach should want him representing their country. What is true is that prior to the Olympics, Shani was not getting what he felt was an appropriate level of coaching from the U.S. team. He went to train in Calgary, where he received amazing treatment, and greatly improved his abilities, mentally and physically, before the Games.

Short track is one of the fastest and most unpredictable sports in the world. Shani had proven himself in the past, had a few rough days and then came back in the 1000-meter trial because he wanted it more than anyone at that particular moment of that particular race. When Shani came off the ice, no official protest was made. No referee stepped in and blew a whistle or approached Shani or any of the other skaters. Susan Ellis walked over to referee Jim Chapin immediately after the event to ask if there had been any disqualifications. All of the refs said the race was fine, as did most of the skaters.

But I didn't know any of these things had happened after the final at the Olympic Trials. I hopped on a plane and flew to L.A. with my father, oblivious to the storm that was brewing.

Haters

"Haters" are people who have nothing better to do in their lives than to focus on rumors, controversy, and alleged mistakes. No matter how good I am, they'll try to find an angle. I'm human like everyone else, but once you get to the top of your sport, or receive a gold medal, people expect you to be flawless. That's impossible. Haters talk about you behind your back. According to them, I'm skating poorly, or using drugs, or running around in a gang. There's nothing I can do about the rumors people start. There's nothing I can do when the media gets frustrated because I won't do controversial interviews and makes up stories or takes things out of context. I am real and I do things straight-up.

I wish it didn't bother me at all. But I really don't like people talking negatively about me. When I was younger, I was pretty confrontational. If I heard someone was talking about me, I went to the source, got in their face, and asked them about it. I can't do that anymore. It just takes me away from my game. I can't pay attention to the stories, because then I wouldn't be concentrating on skating and the haters would win, right?

At the time of the Olympic Trials, I refused to talk with the media about the claims that I helped "fix" a race. The result was a full-on assault by some journalists at a time when I was trying to train for the Games. I read things I never said and quotes I never uttered. Some writers cared about the truth and others cared about selling papers. The latter would throw a smoke bomb in your face just to see if you could find your way out of the haze.

In the last year, I've even watched a coach from a different team whom I've always respected try to win a gold medal at the Olympics despite an obvious disqualification. I've had to question who my friends are, and then question my answers. I know what it feels like to get stabbed in the back, and to helplessly listen to lies and try to rise above the mud. I've attempted to carry myself with class and hope that I've succeeded more than I've failed, because I don't want to turn into one of the haters. Anger and bitterness are poisons, and if anyone swallows too much, they can become bent on others' destruction. Surrounding yourself with family and friends is the only way to avoid haters. People will always be there to shoot you down, but family is there to catch you when you fall.

December 22, following the Olympic Trials, my dad and I flew to L.A. for a Nike photo and commercial shoot. That means we missed the post-trials banquet in Salt Lake City, which is when some rumors about the 1000-meters first started to fly—whispers eventually taking on a life of their own, so that by December 27 they'd become a monster nobody could kill with one blow.

In L.A., Dad and I stayed in a beautiful hotel and went to the shoot where we were part of a revolutionary commercial—the slick Nike one where great music plays in the background while active cuts are made to different athletes in the motion of their sports. I felt fantastic. I'd made it through the trials despite a potentially career-ending back injury that was still causing me some problems. I'd skated smart and protected my position on the team and my chance to compete in each individual event. Everything I'd questioned in the past (like my own abilities), suffered through, and trained for was happening. Plus I was in a fantastic hotel in L.A., surrounded by top athletes and talented photographers.

We started to hear some outrageous rumors at the end of the week, but we had no idea that the "controversy" was taking on a life of its own. I was still worried about my back and so my dad and I flew to see Dr. Lavine in Tacoma, Washington. From there, I went back to Colorado Springs.

I was shocked by the newspaper headlines when I returned to the training center. I was floored by the hundreds of messages from the media on my answering machine asking for interviews and "my side of the story." Funny, I never talked to them but they still printed so many horrible things. I read that Rusty, Shani, and I might be torn off the Olympic team. I watched reporters talk about my losing gold medals before the Games had even begun. *This will blow over,* I told myself. *Get on with training for the Olympics.* There was less than a month before I'd fly to Salt Lake City for the Games. I decided to ignore the rumors and press coverage as best I could and focus on training and my continuing back rehabilitation with Scott.

Unfortunately, one skater's disappointment about not making the Olympic team turned into a tornado and it was reported that I was caught in its eye. In truth, I handled the situation fairly well. I stepped inside of myself, closed the blinds, and shut the door. It took mental strength and probably drained me more than I recognized, but I was tough and resilient and I went about my business.

Shani, Rusty, and I did not fight back. We thought the entire problem would disappear if we didn't lend it any credibility. Plus, I *knew* what had happened and if someone was unhappy and wanted to file a grievance, the system was built to be fair, and the truth would become evident. On December 27, 2001, an official complaint was filed with U.S. Speedskating. Attorney Steve Smith was hired to conduct an inquiry (arbitrator James Holbrook was brought in later). Immediately Kevin Duff, attorney for the complainant, said that because Smith had worked in the past for U.S. Speedskating he couldn't be impartial. A letter was sent to Lloyd Ward, chief executive of the U.S. Olympic Committee asking for the appropriateness of Smith's involvement to be questioned.

The following are official news quotes from the Olympic Trials:

The allegation from a member of the U.S. National Team: That Apolo Anton Ohno and Rusty Smith conspired to allow Ohno's friend, Shani Davis, win the 1000-meter event, thereby earning enough points to make the Olympic team, and to keep Ron Biondo from finishing ahead of Smith, meaning Smith would skate the 1000-meters at the Olympics.

Rusty Smith (excerpts from his ESPN.com diary): With the trials almost over and the Olympic berths already in hand, a more conservative approach than usual was justified. The thing that people don't understand is that you don't always have to win to qualify and it's not worth making a stupid pass and risking injury when you're in a qualifying position. . . . Apolo has won every race, and the last thing he needed to do was go down. . . . Plus, it was incredibly tough to pass Shani. . . . I tried a couple of times and I couldn't get by.

U.S. Speedskating Attorney Steve Smith: My goal is just to get to the truth of what happened. Certainly Apolo has been a dominant skater and he did not win this last race, the question becomes why didn't he win the last race. I want to avoid jumping to conclusions. . . . If you're going to accuse someone of colluding than you need to be sure that it is accurate.

The official (and only) response from Apolo: With a near-fall four laps before the end of the race, I decided to play it safe and protect my place in the 1000-meters for the Olympic Games. I've said since the moment I learned of the accusations that they were untrue and I did nothing wrong. This unfortunate situation and the questioning of my character by a few specific people has been trying. But I am completely focused on winning gold for the U.S. in Salt Lake next month.

Only a month before the 2002 Olympics, I was embroiled in a controversy that put the entire U.S. team under strain and stress and ultimately hurt the sport of short track. But I still refused to give the matter any credence and held off doing interviews. I had tried my best at the Olympic Trials. I won every heat to get to the 500-meter finals and then set an American record in the process of beating J.P. Kepka, Rusty Smith, and Dan Weinstein for the win. I'd secured my places in the 1000-, 5000-meter relay, and 1500-meters the same way—by working hard, playing it smart, and knowing what I had to do to get on the team.

A smart skater and their coach know the point systems for every event and championship. If I have enough points going into a final to come in second or third during a race, I'll probably play it safe and stay in the back like I have many times in the past. If I can avoid hitting the pads or getting sliced up by someone's blade, that's what I'll do. At the Olympic Trials, I was fast but smart. If given the chance to compete at the trials again, I'd play it the same way.

The pressure mounted. The media reported I was the "central figure" in the controversy because I was number one on the U.S. team. It was tough not to let anger enter the situation. I tried to look upon the problem as another test. Life forces always conspire, and it's up to each person to face adversity and push through it. I didn't want to hate the skater who was causing my difficulties. I wanted to rise above his actions and the gossip.

"Shut your ears," my dad said, "and try not to listen to the television or reporters. Focus on the journey and your future."

Meanwhile, the Olympics attorneys and arbitrators were having a preliminary hearing with the roach and his lawyer. Neither myself, Rusty, or Shani were asked to be there. We were never asked to testify during any official hearings because the grievance never got that far despite the attention it received. There was a leak after the preliminary hearing and the media reported that another skater from the U.S. team was corroborating the roach's false allegations. "U.S. gold medal hopefuls," the media said, "might not be going to the 2002 Games." That was totally untrue.

Right up until the end of the controversy, I still didn't want to get involved. I believed that I should remain focused on my training. Shani, Rusty, and I didn't conspire to fix any race. I don't talk to anyone on the day of a competition, especially one as monumental as the Olympic Trials. The morning of the trials I put on my earphones, warmed up on the ice and the bikes, did my heats, and focused inwardly on what I needed to do to improve, skate my best, and get to the finals of each event.

In the end I had to hire a lawyer—a great guy named Chris Cipoletti. He worked to reveal the "significant inconsistencies," in the testimonies that had been heard by U.S. Speedskating. Race witnesses, including race referees, signed affidavits that they heard or saw no behavior indicating the race had been "fixed."

Chris didn't let the scandal drop even when the roach and his attorney withdrew their complaint. He asked that the arbitrator, James Holbrook, issue findings anyway in order to clear the taint now associated with my name. "If we don't do that," Chris explained, "the cloud will still be hanging over speed skating and the athletes."

James Holbrook issued a statement that, "Neither Ohno, Smith, nor Davis violated the rules or code of conduct of the U.S. Speedskating, the USOC, or the International Skating Union. Some statements in the submitted affidavits were admittedly inaccurate and there is no evidence submitted which would support any finding that the race had been fixed."

Something unknown to the media was the conversation my father had at the Olympic Trials with the roach. The skater was upset because he'd fallen behind in points. When he saw my father in the stands, my dad encouraged him—they'd known each other for years and had always been friendly. "You're going to make it," Dad told the roach. "You're a great racer and you'll make up those points." They smiled at each other and the skater left. Dad remembers hoping he'd made a difference in the young man's life. He never thought that same kid would try to hurt his son.

I'd like to write a bit about balance in the wake of the Olympic Trials. My balance, in addition to my ever present, wise, and loyal father, is someone very special to me. I've lived away from home and traveled since I was fourteen and there wasn't a lot of time for dating. In Lake Placid there also wasn't much of a chance to meet anyone I even wanted to date.

Of course I'd wanted to meet someone intelligent, funny, goal-oriented, and attractive for years, but right at the top of my list was also understanding, and that's the toughest attribute to find. My schedule is crazy. If a girl doesn't understand how much I need to travel and the demands of my sport, it'll never work.

Some months, especially after the Olympics, I travel almost every day with multiple appearances, events, and competitions. There's no moment to spare between each, and there are days I can't even make a phone call because I'm doing interviews in the car on the way to a race or having meetings with sponsors or agents between appearances. At night I'm asleep before I hit the pillow. I can't feel guilty about achieving my goals or potential. Right now skating is at the forefront of my life, and I believe that's what separates elite athletes from everyday people.

Unlike a banker or attorney, I have a limited career life. Most skaters don't have long careers because the young guys start shooting them down and have more strength and endurance, and because accidents in training and on the ice put so much wear and tear on your body that eventually you're eliminated from the top ranks. I truly believe that I'm going to be a tough contender for as long as I'm skating. If my results start to drop, I'll get out of the game. My dad always stresses that I'm so young I have tons of years left in the sport. He wants to make certain I use this time well, meet lots of people and don't tie myself down. He knows what happens to life once you complicate it with marriage and children. But I'm nineteen and those decisions have to be mine.

I met a very special person in the summer of 2001. She didn't know who I was, much about the sport of short track or anything about the Olympic Trials. We first talked at a friend's house, and a bit over the phone after that. Eventually we went dancing at some clubs and started spending more and more time together. We just clicked, and she brought out a different side of me. Before her I was all about training. Now I have more of a balance, and I'm a lot happier. Not just because she puts up with my schedule or because she leaves me notes and messages or just comes by to say hello. She has a fiery personality and is her own person. If anyone confronts her, she fights back (a lot like me). She's the strongest woman I've ever met in my life, and she helps me understand myself. Maybe because I didn't have a mother, she shows me a different side of life and I admire her.

When my stardom happened after the Olympics nothing changed in our close relationship. Much like my dad, she has never treated me differently. She still likes to drive to the mountains at night and watch the stars for hours. So do I. She doesn't care about "Apolo the short track gold medalist"; she cares about me. The past few years have been filled with tough life lessons about trust and false friendships, and learning to both respect and sometimes fear the power of the media, but I still let a new person into my life, which makes me feel proud because at this point it's counterintuitive. I trusted her and I'll always feel blessed by our relationship. She's not one of the haters, and I try to live up to her expectations, which makes me a better man.

Silver, Rounding the Last Corner

The Olympics are the pinnacle of sports—there's nothing else like them. They are the number-one competition of all time and the chance to get on the podium is slim to none. Athletes train all of their lives for the single chance to compete in the Games and since they only happen every four years the planning that goes into making it to the top during that window is mind-numbing. World-class Olympic athletes are a special breed because we're amateurs—we're not getting paid. It's extremely tough to reach the top of your sport, and the chance to compete at the Olympics for your country is a phenomenal once-in-a-lifetime experience and that's why we're all there. There's nothing similar in professional athletics because we represent the purest form of sports, and training four years for a single competition magnifies its importance.

Flying into Salt Lake City for the Games was unreal. The airport was packed with athletes retrieving enormous colorful bags of gear, coaches directing their teams to waiting buses, reporters zipping around the terminal looking for stories, and armed members of the military in camouflage with large guns hoisted over their shoulders. Security was incredibly tight but I appreciated it. There was a checkpoint for everything I did from the moment I arrived at the Games.

Before teams were allowed to enter the Olympic Village, we had to do a lot of paperwork to get our identification and passes. It was so hard to focus on filling out the appropriate forms when athletes from around the world, the elite of their sports, were buzzing about next to me. I just wanted to look at everyone and everything. But I also wanted to get my official Olympic identification cards and go shopping.

That's what it feels like when you receive your official Olympic garb—a big free shopping trip. You're taken through several armed checkpoints to an enormous warehouse. I was given a shopping cart and told to follow the lines painted on the floor through each row. People handed me coats, hats, T-shirts, pants, sweaters, socks, sunglasses, underwear, sneakers . . . you name it, all with the Olympic insignia and the letters *U.S.A.* With my cart overflowing, I proceeded through checkout and then filled my arms with all my free stuff, both walking and riding through several more checkpoints before entering the Olympic Village.

The Olympic Village is a pretty normal-looking place—dorms, athletic facilities, and a sports medicine center. But if you look around, there are athletes from every country in the world eating in the cafeteria or going for a run in their own official Olympic clothing. A part of me wanted to talk to all the other athletes and learn from them, but I'd come too far to be distracted.

Opening night ceremonies for the Salt Lake City 2002 Winter Olympics were indescribable . . . once we got inside the arena. I waited in a line of thousands of athletes outside the packed stadium while fifty-two thousand (it sounded like a hundred thousand) people waited inside for the ceremony to begin. It was winter in Utah, so despite the warm clothing we were given, if you stood in the same place for hours, you got cold. I got really cold and couldn't seem to shake off the chills. Still, I didn't let that ruin the experience.

After the official events, including the United States' heart-pounding procession around the stadium, the entertainment began.

The theme of the performances was "Light the Fire Within," and the show was an extravaganza of music, special effects, and incredible performances. The Dixie Chicks, LeAnn Rimes, and Native American performers Rita Coolidge and Walela performed. Sting was also there, and so were composer-performer Robbie Robertson and cellist Yo-Yo Ma. A local a cappella group called Eclipse and a folk group, The Deseret String Band/Bunkhouse Orchestra played along with the Mormon Tabernacle Choir and the Utah Symphony.

The special effects blew me away. Hundreds of fiber optics embedded in the ice looked like stars; five circular electric-powered platforms carried performers across the stadium floor and clouds of fog floated through the air. The skaters put on a beautiful performance and it was hard to know where to look next because there was one surprise after another. I just stared in disbelief because I was there, a part of the live opening ceremonies, one of the athletes who had earned the right to compete in the Olympics.

Three and a half billion people tuned in to the opening ceremonies and they definitely got an unforgettable show. What I got was a ton of attention and interviews, my face on the gigantic screen above the stadium, and the flu.

I honestly believe that no one at the opening ceremonies would have known my name if it hadn't been for NBC's coverage of short track in the months prior to the 2002 Games. Their reporters were always fair, and though they could have focused solely on the controversy at the trials, they chose a different road and I admire them for that.

NBC profiled many athletes before the Games, and they did a great job on my profile, allowing me to move forward in my training and efforts to do well at the Games. I believe that NBC literally set the direction for Olympics coverage and the rest of the media followed. I'm very thankful to Johnson McKelvy, who did the piece on me and has been so instrumental in my positive relationship with NBC.

In addition NBC treated my father like a king. Most parents of skaters are not afforded good seats at competitions, especially at the Olympic Games. The federation had given my dad tickets in the nose-bleed section, where he would have to watch me skate on the giant monitors because he couldn't see clearly all the way down to the ice. He would feel more like a spectator than part of my Olympic experience—*our* experience because we are a team.

My dad was a big part of why I had the chance to race at the Games, so the idea of him not being close to the action was pretty wack. NBC found my father and brought him down to their broadcasting booth, right off the ice. He was invited to watch the entire Games from the booth, where he could hear the hiss of the blades, feel the wind off the pack, and share in moments of disappointment and triumph by being the first in line to hug his son.

The flu. That's what I caught four days before my first competition at the 2002 Salt Lake City Olympics. Fever, chills, sore throat, vomiting. My upper respiratory system was totally wacked out. I was moved from the Olympic Village, where the athletes stay for the Games, to a hotel that was closer to the Delta Center . . .

So why is this happening to me? *I wondered as I lay in bed with the flu four days before my first Salt Lake City Olympic event, the 1000-meter preliminaries. My mind raced . . . I was healthy the day before. My back was feeling better. I was finally at the Olympics after years of fighting illnesses and injuries. Why is this happening? This is the Olympics and athletes are showing everything they've got. With only three months of extremely weak training I'd made it to the Games, but I was sick when I was supposed to be at my best.*

The doctors offered to give me antibiotics. They were necessary at that point, but they're never a cure for me. My body isn't used to drugs, so I react strongly to antibiotics. They make me tired and slow, and basically I can't even get out of bed the next day. Four days before Wednesday's preliminary trials, where I would have to place well in order to get into the Saturday 1000-meter Olympic finals, all I wanted to do was sleep, and I had trouble walking to the bathroom without sniffling, watering eyes, and dizziness. Apolo Anton Ohno, the supposed big threat in short track skating, was being brought to his knees by wracking coughs, fever, and a shot of antibiotics in his ass.

My father stepped in to help me with my program of hydration and detoxification, but I improved slowly, not in leaps and bounds. Still, by the time of the prelims I was on the upswing. I forgot about the flu the moment I walked into the packed arena.

The noise was deafening. Tens of thousands of fans had come to watch short track, and because of NBC's coverage they knew my name and chanted it over and over again. There was a sea of supportive signs that I wish I'd had time to read. I felt a tremendous surge of energy, but tried to keep my cool. When I stepped onto the ice, I had trouble hearing myself think, and the cheering made my ears buzz and my teeth chatter. There was no time to consider the last few days. It simply was not a question anymore of whether I was ready—I was going to skate, and I was there to compete well. I put my head down and did what I had to do, qualifying through my preliminaries and heats. By the time I returned to the hotel, I was slated to race on Saturday.

I have never experienced a race like the 1000-meter final. Though many people look at it and say, "Well, that's short track," it's not true. I have never witnessed or been involved in a race like that one; never. This time I was ready for the electricity of the crowd and after a moment of appreciation, I used the cheers as energy and tuned out the noise. The lineup was fierce—China's Jiajun Li, Canada's Mathieu Turcotte, South Korea's Hyun-Soo Ahn, and Australia's Steven Bradbury. I got off the line well, reserving my strength and drafting off the front skaters until I was ready to make my move. With four laps to go, I was in perfect position and started to surge. At two laps I pulled into the lead in front of Ahn. The fans went into a frenzy and their energy was like a bolt of electricity. I pushed harder and was seconds away from winning the race.

On the final turn Li attempted an outside pass, tangling arms with me and slowing my speed. He fell, slid into the pads, and eventually was disqualified. Since I'd slowed, Ahn tried to pass on the inside, even though there was no room. He fell too, and his right hand grabbed at my left leg in a last-ditch effort to stay on his feet. The grab sent me into a spin and I landed on my backside before crashing into the wall.

Sometimes, if I'm about to pull off a crazy move as I'm going down, a fall will occur in slow motion. There was no slow motion during this fall. I went down fast and hit hard. My head slammed into the pads and then ricocheted off. During the fall I caught my left inner thigh with my own blade and gashed my leg, but didn't even notice it at the time. Turcotte had also been taken out by Ahn and lay on the ice beside me. Steven Bradbury of Australia, who'd been in the back, well over ten meters behind the pack, skated across the finish line and won as the "last man standing."

I don't know what possessed me to scramble to my feet, to fall yet again and then rise, my leg numb from the wound and slick with blood that pooled to the edge of my skate and puddled inside. Maybe it was instinct . . . I don't know . . .

NBC had cameras both on the 1000-meter race and my father's face, waiting for him to register the thrill of victory or the agony of defeat. The crash in the final lap was spectacular, but my dad had seen crashes before. There have been times when I couldn't walk off the ice, so the fact that I was moving at all after hitting the wall was a huge relief to him. But when I struggled to my feet, Dad said I managed to surprise even him.

My bell had definitely been rung from the impact of the wall, my head felt too light and my ears hummed. I could hear the crowd screaming but couldn't make out any words. I pushed myself to my feet. Turcotte, seeing me move, leaped up, despite his own painful cut. I struggled forward, willing myself across the finish line. I won the silver medal and Turcotte, just a breath behind me, won the bronze.

I felt unbelievably proud. I went out there and skated one of the best races of my life. There's never a guarantee of who is going to win, and I never ever, ever take a race for granted until I cross the finish line. When I fell, I just wanted to finish the race. I did more than that. I *won* the silver. My father was the first to hug me when I stepped off the ice. He followed me to the sports medicine area to get my leg treated because the blood had soaked through my suit. I received six stitches from the doctor, and Eric Heiden, now a physician, was in the room at the time, which was pretty cool.

In a wheelchair to help take the weight off my leg, I quickly returned to the ice for the medal ceremony. I wasn't going to receive a medal sitting down if I could help it, and hopped onto the podium with a huge smile and my arms raised in victory. When the silver medal was hung around my neck I took a moment to close my eyes, tilt my head back, and be thankful.

Bradbury said later about his gold medal, "It's good, but it doesn't feel right you know. I wasn't as strong as the other guys out there, but I'm going to take it. I consider myself the luckiest man. This is my day." In response, I say that on that day, at that given moment, he was the strongest guy out there *and* the only one left standing. I performed under extreme circumstances and skated the best race of my life. I gave 110 percent until the very end.

There were thousands of fans that thought my 1000-meter race should be run again; that I *deserved* the gold medal. I could easily have been taken along for the ride, believing them because of my own selfish desires. There is always a temptation for athletes to ride the current of public perception. The 2002 Games taught me some valuable lessons about the power of opinion, as in the situation with the Canadian pairs skating event. In that case unfair judging was at play, and eventually a double gold medal ceremony was performed. But the discovery about the judge whose scores were swayed wouldn't have been made if the public hadn't been outraged and demanded answers. In the case of the 1000-meter finals, I *knew* that I'd won the silver—I was ecstatic about it and satisfied with the fairness of the event as the decision of the referees not to rerun the race was theirs to make, not mine. As an athlete my job is to come prepared the best I can, mentally and physically, to skate hard giving 110 percent and to walk away feeling satisfied.

I didn't come to the Olympics for four gold medals. I struggled and faced every challenge and test to get to the Games because I believe it is all part of my journey. Some people work toward getting rich, others want to be stronger, faster, smarter, better looking. If I have just one goal, then when I reach it my life will be over. My journey is always about getting to a place, then passing and surpassing it with the next trip. There's no ultimate destination—it's the journey that I love.

After the 1000-meter finals, my father received this forwarded e-mail from James Holbrook (arbitrator during the Olympic Trials controversy):

> *Apolo Ohno's humble and gracious remarks last night reflect great credit on himself, his sport, his team, and our country. I know you are justifiably proud of this remarkable young man.*

My dad told me that one of the most precious moments of his life was witnessing the way I handled the finals and winning the silver medal. "A parent can only hope that everything they've tried to instill in their son about winning, losing, facing trials, controversy, and stumbling blocks, will be understood. When you stepped onto the podium to receive your silver medal, I was unbelievably proud of who you'd become."

Gold

"**R**eady for the next one?" That's what every friend, skater, coach, doctor, and psychologist said to me after the 1000-meter final. I was on crutches, my thigh was bandaged and swollen from the stitches, and I was wondering if the deep gash was going to hurt my chances to get to the finals for the 1500-meter event. If I was too explosive, the stitches would rip free during the race. If I wasn't, I'd never get to the finals. "Ready for the next one?" *Don't you see that I'm in pain, on crutches, wounded?* "Ready for the next one?" *Ugggh*. I lay in bed for a whole day after winning the silver medal because I couldn't train or go for a run. I only had three days before the 1500-meter event.

Dr. Lavine was still in Salt Lake City and instead of taking another shot of antibiotics to ensure I wouldn't get an infection from the cut, I decided to have him work on me. I just couldn't afford the negative reaction to the medicine and I would rather have been in pain than to be slow and groggy. Everyone was skeptical except for my father, who believes in the power of alternative medicine. Three days later, my swelling had gone down and there was no sign of an infection. My leg felt a little bit stiff, but I knew that I was ready to skate. I easily passed through the preliminary races and made it to the 1500-meter short track finals.

A lot of traffic. That's what I thought when I exploded off the starting line near the front of the pack in the 1500 finals—six skaters and a lot of traffic. I decided to hang out toward the back, watching the other skaters and biding my time, which was very risky, especially at the Games. Marc Gagnon was in the lead, but early on Dong-Sung bumped me on an outside pass and burst all the way to the front of the group. Suddenly I was exactly where Dong-Sung wanted me to be, in last place, because in his eyes I was his biggest competition. He started picking up the pace because he knew that it would be extremely hard for me to pass four guys in order to get to him.

I tried to move up but there was no room. With five laps to go, I couldn't find a gap and everyone was fighting to stay in front of me. *Relax,* I told myself. *There will be an opportunity.* In the second to last lap, I made a three-skater pass on the inside, surging into second place behind Kim. I could hear the South Korean short track coach, Myung-Kyu Jon, who we call "Big Jon," yelling to Kim that I was on his heels. *That's okay,* I thought. *Let him know I'm here and feeling strong.*

Big Jon has been coaching for over fourteen years, has eight world champions, and handfuls of Olympic gold medals. He's been around the block, knows how to coach, and something he's doing over in South Korea is bringing the best out of skaters. Plus he speaks six languages—Korean, Japanese, English, French, Italian, and Chinese. Some say his style is unorthodox, but no one really knows because no one in Korea is allowed to watch his athletes practice.

When I first started to skate, I really respected Big Jon. Even when I was too stubborn to listen to my dad or my own coach, I'd sidle up to him at competitions and ask questions about different athletes and their strengths and weaknesses. As soon as I got good, Big Jon stopped talking to me, but I still appreciated him as a great coach and understood that he didn't want to help me beat his skaters.

When the bell rang for the final lap of the race, I began to make an inside pass to get by Dong-Sung and into first place. I was totally focused—I knew that I had enough strength and power left to beat the South Korean because I'd been able to draft for half the race while he was forced to maintain his lead position. I set myself up to come around the last inside corner really tight, but Dong-Sung moved over on me, blocking my path (cross-tracking).

We were a breath away from colliding at high speed when instinctively I pulled back my arms, my hands raised to chest level to ward off the blow. I was certain what was coming—we were going to crash, hit the ice and slam into the pads. At the very least, even though it was Dong-Sung who hit me, I might be disqualified for impeding another skater's progress (you never know what a referee will think he sees). Or I'd have to slow so much that the skaters behind me would pass by, leaving me in the back of the pack with too much distance to recover in too little time. Somehow Dong-Sung and I didn't collide and I crossed the finish line behind him, in second place.

Tony, the U.S. assistant coach, immediately shot his arm into the air, waving over the referee. I looked at Big Jon and our eyes met. Pat Maxwell, another great coach who I was working with at the Games, said to Big Jon, "Jon, that's a blatant cross-track." Big Jon said nothing. He glanced at my coach, then at me again, and his arms shot into the air in a victory sign. Despite what had occurred on the track, Big Jon was not going to acknowledge the possibility of disqualification. He sent Dong-Sung on a victory lap, and the skater held South Korea's flag high, circling the ice. I slowly circled too, waiting for the official call that I expected to be in my favor.

On the ice, I waited through the longest minute of my life. *Are they going to call it?* I was thrilled to win the silver in the 1000-meters, but this time I knew that I'd *won* the gold. Referee James Hewish of Australia signaled that Dong-Sung's cross-tracking move had obstructed me during the race and he was disqualified. It was a fair call that was on the way to being made even before Tony motioned the referee over. Dong-Sung threw his own nation's flag to the ground in apparent disgust.

❄ ❄ ❄

There was only enough time to leap off the ice into my father's arms for his whispered words of congratulations before racing to change my clothes. "They can just throw me in the desert and bury me. I got a gold medal. I'm good now," I told reporters as I raced back to the edge of the ice in time to hear my name called out as the "gold medal winner of the men's 1500-meter final."

This time I wasn't limping as I ascended the podium to the top step. When the medal was hung around my neck, I clasped my hands, giving a prayer of thanks, and then held the gold medal in the air while the fans cheered so loud that I felt the ground beneath my feet shake. I looked over to my dad, who was crying, and silently thanked him for never giving up on me. When the United States anthem played, I quietly sang along. Seeing the American flag get raised, hearing the crowd go crazy, feeling the weight of a gold medal around my neck was a dream come true. I invited silver medalist Jiajun Li and bronze medalist Marc Gagnon, two champions in their own right, onto the top step so that we could all share the moment together.

My dad was beside himself that night. He stayed at the hotel with me and I showed him the gold medal. He held it, but wouldn't hang it around his neck. He recalled watching me grow up surrounded by the ocean and wind, wanting to teach me everything; he remembered the moment when I started to rebel and he felt like his flesh and blood had turned against him. Every parent, he said, goes through the anguish of their child's teenage years and hopes for the best. He had seen each struggle and every disappointment and lived through them with me. Now he had gotten to watch me jump up and down in pure joy. For my dad, that was what it had all been about.

In my mind, there were no more controversies. I had skated the two best races of my life and whether I won gold or silver wasn't the point. I'd performed well under the spotlight and despite every challenge. I was extremely happy, because I'd gone out there and done my best, giving 110 percent. I didn't hear that the South Koreans were protesting the race until the next day. Their team was supposed to dominate in the Games, but the men's team had yet to win any medals. That must have been tough for the skaters and especially for Big Jon, who was used to always winning.

South Korea made an appeal against Dong-Sung's disqualification to the Court of Arbitration for Sport (CAS). They also appealed to the International Olympic Committee (IOC) over the results. The CAS tribunal met two days later and after reviewing the tapes, talking to referees, witnesses, and other skaters, upheld the disqualification. The IOC agreed with the ruling.

Fabio Carta, in support of the South Korean team, was quoted as saying "We should use a rifle on Ohno." When later asked by reporters if he wanted to withdraw his comment in such a tight security event as the Olympics and given the violent world situation and the September 11 tragedy, Carta declined.

A few days later Carta tried to speak to me. I said no. His team members continued to approach me, asking if Carta could have a moment of my time. I finally relented. Carta explained to me that the media had taken everything he'd said out of context. When he said that "we should use a rifle on Ohno," he'd meant that in his country when a skater is so strong and so fast, you need a bolt of lightning to stop him. I gave Carta the benefit of the doubt and accepted his apology. I had races to skate.

Unfortunately that wasn't the end of things. The Olympic Village received thousands of e-mails from upset fans and the sheer number crashed their server. People weren't just writing in support of Dong-Sung, they were writing that they disliked me. It felt truly horrible to know that so many fans of short track didn't understand that I'd fairly won the gold medal. (Later, I was relieved to learn that it was only a couple of guys sending all those e-mails.)

I called my friend Dave Creswell. We'd maintained contact even though he'd moved to UCLA to get his Ph.D. in sports psychology. I'd called him after my back injury for advice and he'd helped me brainstorm goals and how to structure a negative experience into something positive. We also spoke right after the Olympics opening ceremony, when I'd gotten sick and he'd suggested I insulate myself from chaos and distractions and get back in the bathtub each night to practice my breathing and meditation. But this was bigger.

Dave thought I was phoning because I'd just won a gold medal in the Olympics. I usually called him for damage control, so he was thrilled I was calling to tell him I'd done well. I told him about the crazed fans not liking me because I'd won gold over South Korea's best.

Instantly realizing he was still on damage control, Dave thought about his answer before he spoke. "Can you put yourself in the Korean fans' shoes?" he asked, in his typical fashion of never giving me an easy answer and shifting the responsibility back onto my own shoulders.

"Yeah," I replied, "but I'd never act so crazy like that."

"Can you do anything about how they feel?"

"Not really. Just skate my best and continue to show my honor and integrity."

"Well then, I guess that's what you should do," Dave said.

Dave's no-nonsense attitude is one of the reasons I've continued to work with him through the years. My mental training involves new awareness, and learning how to work as a member of a team and in the position of leader, by virtue of my standings in the short track world and my personality, which tends toward taking on that role (even though I don't always like it). Dave challenges me to take the most from others and to understand that when competitors skate faster, it brings my performance to a new level. On a daily basis, I work on embracing challenges and using them to build more concentration, focus, and diligence in every aspect of my training.

❋ ❋ ❋

I turned my focus toward the 500-meter competition. I felt horrible. The stitches on my thigh were hurting, and with the explosive start needed to win the 500-meter race, I wasn't sure they'd hold together. I was also bone tired. Still, I got up the next day, went to the arena, suited up, put on my best game face, and skated onto the ice.

During my second semifinal of the event, I got off to an extremely slow start and hung in the back until the third lap of the four-and-a-half-lap race. In third place, I made a move to catch Satoru Terao from Japan. I had more power than I thought and quickly ran up on him. I've read articles that said that my outside blade caught the Japanese skater and upended him, sending him careening into the pads. Some wrote that I knocked into Terao while trying to pass him. The angles on the videotapes are unclear. The truth is, I was waiting, waiting, waiting to pass. I set up the Japanese skater so I could pass on the inside. I tried to hold the track and ran out of room. Terao was wide in the corner and so light that I think he was already going down when I brushed past him. I put up my arm so we wouldn't collide, which looks like a push from some angles on the video, but I was just trying to protect myself.

I finished the race in third, then circled the ice waiting to see if there were going to be any rulings. I glanced at the video board, hoping to catch a replay. The call came in—I was disqualified. In the end Terao was given a spot in the final, but finished last of the five skaters. Rusty Smith took the bronze for the United States, Jonathan Guilmette of Canada took silver, and his teammate Marc Gagnon claimed the gold—his first individual gold. I was happy for all of them—they're great skaters—and especially for Rusty, who is a friend and such a hard worker.

The last Olympic short track event was the 5000-meter relay. I thought the United States had a big chance to win the final. Our strategy was to stay in front and do everything right. The Canadians started off in first place, with China in second. But when they made their exchange of skaters, Li clashed skates with Gagnon and both skaters went down. Gagnon recovered quickly. A few seconds later a skater from the Italian team went down. It looked like it was going to be a fight between the United States and Canada for the gold. But with twenty-six laps to go, Rusty hit a block and took a fall.

Everyone on the Olympic short track team has fallen during a relay. It's a long race that requires mind-numbing timing and, at the Olympics, exerts incredible pressure. I told reporters later that there was "no doubt in my mind if we wouldn't have gone down and I was there in the end, I could have done some magic. But that's just how it is." Rusty felt terrible, but he's an experienced skater and knows it could have happened to any of us.

Dan Weinstein said after the race, "It doesn't change the fact that I think we're still the best relay team in the world. You lose distance, and it's harder to get your speed back after a fall, but you give it everything you have. We were fried at the end. All of us understand. These things can happen." The relay was something we all could learn from because we were strong enough to finish hard and at least get a bronze medal, but we were so focused on the gold that we let the fall drain us and didn't medal at all.

At the end of the 5000 relay, Canada won gold; Italy came in a half lap back for the silver, followed by China for the bronze. Reporters asked if I was disappointed. For the team, yes, because we had high expectations. For myself, no. I came to the Olympics and I did an excellent job, I told them. So many people supported me, all my friends and family were in the stands, and that's just an unbelievable feeling. My first Games and I got two medals; there's nothing better than that.

※ ※ ※

The aftermath of the Olympics was fantastic. Following the relay I went back to the hotel and slept. But as soon as I woke, life clicked over to a frenetic high-speed ride. The closing ceremonies were a spectacular of music, special effects, and fireworks. When the Olympic torch was blown out it felt like the packed stadium and athletes had exhaled in fulfillment.

My father and I were scheduled to go to the NBC studios for an interview right after the Games ended. Security was still extremely tight and guards carrying guns surrounded the chauffeur-driven car. When we reached the car, soldiers opened the hood to check the engine for tampering. It was a very quiet, serious experience. They used mirrors to check for bombs beneath the vehicle. Two policemen stood beside the left-hand door as we climbed in. They asked for our identification badges and we handed them over. My dad and I were kind of freaked by all the guns and silence—it was no time to crack a joke.

Suddenly the right-hand door of the car flew open and one of the soldiers peered in and saw my face. "Apolo," he practically yelled, "we're so proud of you! We've been watching everything you've done and we are one hundred percent behind you!" I was shocked and amazed, thankful, and slightly embarrassed by how much attention the soldier and all of his friends gave me.

The commissioner from the Utah Department of Public Safety personally gave me an official sheriff's jacket and star (the same one given to the president of the United States). The irony of that situation did not pass me by. If you believed what some of the media wrote, I was supposed to be a gang-involved, tough rebellious kid. What's a kid like that doing earning the respect of law enforcement?

I'm only nineteen years old, but I have something to say about dreams, life's challenges, and the rewards of the journey. It's not about winning or losing, it's about continuing to play the game, even when you're so broken down that it feels like it's impossible. Don't get mad; don't get even; get stronger, faster, and more powerful. Fill yourself with knowledge and empathy and an indomitable spirit, because no one else can do that for you. In the end it's your life, your choice, and your world. Give 110 percent, always.

When the Olympics ended, I took some time to remember the struggles, enjoy my successes, and to individually thank everyone who had supported me in my pursuit. The only things that are a certainty for me are the love of my father and friends; my belief that if I fall, I'm going to get back up; and the knowledge that you lose a lot more than you win as a competitive athlete and in life. That's how you learn, and if you don't lose, you'll never really win . . . guaranteed.

Epilogue

You should not ask if you will succeed or not. That isn't what matters the most. The only thing that matters is your struggle to carry it further. God reckons that—the assault—to our account and nothing else. Whether we win or lose is His affair, not ours.

—Nikos Kazantzakis

Fame is a strange cat. Anybody in the world can be famous if they have done something special. Businessmen make great deals and tons of money and people recognize a lot of their names. My job is to be an athlete, and I won two Olympic medals. It's what I do for work. God gives everyone a gift, and it's up to each person to figure out how and if they want to use it. I've been blessed to find my path and give it 110 percent without looking back.

Being recognized is part of fame. As soon as NBC started to focus airtime on me, I couldn't go outside without attracting big crowds that followed me around Salt Lake City and into restaurants where they watched me order and eat. I tried not to drop any food or dribble my water while I ate beneath the watchful stares of hundreds of eyes. Looking around, I wanted to explain to everyone that I was just like them. I'd been in high school (and graduated on time); I went to swim, karate, and skating practices; I just happened to get to the elite level of my sport.

As a famous person, you're under the microscope. The media is sometimes like a snake, wiggling into dark holes and finding out every little thing about you for public consumption. If they're not sneaking around, they're hounding you, and they're relentless when they want your story. The media are the fastest athletes in the world—they're the sprinters, and they rush to put you down or bring you up. They put out countless stories and they have mad endurance.

When I talk to the media, I always try to be genuine. I imagine the audience I'm talking to back home—the people watching from their couches. That helps tremendously because I can be straight-up and try to push away the discomfort of the fact that I'm talking on television and everything I say, right or wrong, is being recorded and shot to millions of viewers. I try to remember that every interview I do is for the fans. They supported me all the way, and I owe them a piece of my success. If the stands had been empty at the Olympics, I would not have been able to skate as well because the air wouldn't have been full of an electric charge or that almost palpable expectation. . . . And yet I must admit that I still get a little nervous.

Sometimes I wonder who I was before the Olympics versus after the Games. I'm still the guy who lives across the street, the one you say hello to at the grocery store. I'm the same inside and I don't say any fake bull when my face is in front of the camera. But now I'm "famous" and have celebrity status. I've been called an "icon." And that does change things.

I don't always know who to trust anymore. I'm not sure if people are being genuine or if they want something from me. People treat me differently now. Most of them are just honest fans who want to talk for a few minutes. I like to meet them and sign autographs for their spouse or kids. Sometimes I get ripped off and see something I signed being auctioned off on eBay for personal gain, but I like to think those cases are few and far between.

❄ ❄ ❄

Today I'm constantly asked if my fame has led me to be a role model for kids. My answer is always that I think kids need a role model, whether it's me or someone else doesn't matter, as long as they have someone. It's an honor at age twenty to even be considered for something like that. I wish I had more of a chance to really get to talk to kids, because they need all the guidance they can get and I think I could help because I know how tough it can be.

I've thought about the positive things I can do with my fame, and I'd like to travel around the country as a speaker, maybe in junior high schools. That's really the age bracket where children can start to go down the wrong path, but it's still early enough that they can change their lives. I want to tell kids what I did when I was younger. It's important for them to understand that I think it's cool to be smart and in an honors program, and that I believe it's vitally important to finish high school and continue education at a higher level. It used to be if you were focused on school you were a geek or a nerd, but that's not true anymore.

There are gangs in Nebraska and New Hampshire and Oregon, and while I flirted with trouble, I want children to see that ultimately I steered clear of the gangs because I couldn't fulfill my promise if I'd gotten sucked into violence and illegal activities. Being powerful within a neighborhood or school and having money, nice things, and respect is cool, but if it's not based on intelligence and personality, it usually doesn't last and it's just a front.

Every kid goes through phases, whether they're wealthy or poor, get picked on by other kids or their siblings, or have troubled parents. I have friends who were in gangs who are now clean-cut professionals. I have friends who are in prison and I don't get the chance to talk to them very much. The thing is, their prior lifestyle had no control, no rules, and now they're living in a cement cell with bars and being told when to eat, sleep, even take a leak. It's ironic that they have absolutely no control in their lives when that's what they thought they were fighting for when they were younger.

My point is that it's important for kids to understand it's normal to hang out with all different kinds of people, but somewhere along the line, before things start to get too serious, they have to make a choice about the direction of their lives. If they think gangs and trouble are the answer, then they need to understand the dreams they'll be forced to give up to achieve that.

Sometimes parents ask me for advice about their kids, especially since the 2002 Games. "Be supportive," I tell them. Kids are going to be kids and parents need to try to be a part of their lives, no matter how bad it gets. If they let the gap in their relationship get too big, they're going to lose their child. A kid will push you farther and farther away until they no longer have interest in you. And once they do, you've lost the opportunity to be a part of their life forever.

One of the greatest opportunities I received as a result of the 2002 Games was the chance to go to an Oscar party in Los Angeles at the invitation of Elton John. Originally I was scheduled to go to the 2002 World Championships in Montreal, Canada. I sent my regrets for the Oscar party, knowing that my responsibility was to my sport. I returned from the Games to Colorado Springs and continued my training, even though most of the skaters went home for a break, and I had to train alone.

It's not unusual for an Olympic gold medalist to entirely skip the World Championships, but I felt compelled to race. While training I reinjured a previously hurt ankle, rolling and spraining it again. I went to see my osteopath, Dr. Lavine, and after examining me, he advised that I shouldn't compete and sent a letter to Fred Benjamin, head of the federation, documenting my injury. Since I had to take time off from training, on a whim I decided to see if that invitation for the Oscar party was still open. In all honesty things worked out for the best. I needed a break, bad. I didn't feel prepared to compete again after four long years of training, and I needed some distance from the sport.

Attending Elton John's party was one of the most exciting experiences of my life. I met Halle Berry and Elton John, and saw Oscar winner Denzel Washington. Many of the actors, producers, and directors actually came up to meet me! They thanked me for my hard work, and for winning medals for America. I ate incredible food and stared at the famous people wandering by. Dave Creswell stared too, because I'd brought him along to the party to thank him for all his support over the years.

That night, between the celebrity sightings and introductions, Dave and I talked about my Olympic experience. "It's the tip of the iceberg," I told him. "I can do so much more." I was truly elated, and the chance to share such a unique and fun experience with Dave made it all the better.

The media reported that I had withdrawn from the World Championships in order to attend an Oscar party. The stories made me sound shallow and pretentious and disinterested in my sport. I've given everything to short track and I'd hoped for a little bit more respect.

Right after the Games I flew to L.A. to do my first big late-night talk show appearance. I went into the bathroom in Leno's green room to shave before the show. I didn't have a razor so someone found a nasty old blade for me. I must have cut myself fifty times. There were red dots of blood all over my face and the nicks wouldn't stop bleeding.

Outside the bathroom door, I heard Jay enter the green room. He asked where I was because he wanted to hang out with me before the show. After a few minutes Jay called out, "Apolo, what are you doing in there? Are you scared? Don't you want to come out to meet me?"

"Oh, I'm just shaving," I said through the door.

"Don't cut yourself," Jay joked.

I went into the green room with little dabs of toilet paper all over my face. Jay thought it was hysterical—he was dying laughing. The makeup people put Vaseline on my cuts to stop the bleeding. I looked okay when I went onstage, but Jay busted me right away.

"Why don't you tell everybody in the stands what you were doing in the back and how many times you cut yourself shaving?" Jay suggested.

I was embarrassed—even more so because there were a lot of female fans in the audience screaming like I was a Backstreet Boy. It was the first time I realized my popularity with girls and though I felt shy, I have to admit it beat the alternative. After Leno, I went on the Conan O'Brien show. That guy is really tall and straight-up crazy, on and off the air. He was nice and real and I had a great time.

My next big appearance was on the *Rosie O'Donnell Show*. I didn't get to meet Rosie until I went onstage. She treated me like a king. "You're almost as cute as Tom Cruise . . . cute boy, cute car," Rosie said, handing me a set of keys to a brand-new car—a gift from Rosie to me!

The post-Olympic moments didn't stop with the car. I was invited to be a guest on MTV's TRL *(Total Request Live)* in Times Square. That was definitely cool. I hung out at the studio for the afternoon, introducing videos and taking questions. Carson heard I knew how to break dance and he called me out on the spot. MTV started playing music and even though I felt shy, I got out there and did a windmill spin on my shoulders and neck. The fans in the studio and down on the street went wild, screaming and waving signs. I was more nervous to do TRL than any other appearance because many of my friends watch that show.

✳ ✳ ✳

By far one of the craziest things I did after the Olympics was a shoot for *W* magazine in the Dominican Republic with famous photographer Bruce Weber. I brought Dave down for the shoot—just another way to say thanks for all his hard work and also because he's a great friend and I like having him around.

The shoot was in a very small town. I remember looking around at the level of poverty and still seeing tons of smiling faces. The streets were filthy, smelled like exotic food combined with manure and old fish, and there were tons of flies. The kids, dressed in ragged clothing, ran around carrying foul buckets of brown-gray water, trying to wash all of our shoes. I gave them some spare change for the kind thought. What struck me most about the village where we shot and those kids, was that the people were very poor, but still happy with life.

Cheryl Tiegs and a few top baseball players were part of the four-day shoot. Across the board, *W* put us in some crazy clothing. We did a lot of shots in knee-deep water and Bruce was fantastic to work with—he's got an amazing eye and he's like an athlete in the zone. Sometimes I'd just hang around and watch him take pictures. When we were shooting, we learned that former President Clinton and his family happened to be in town. I had the chance to spend some time with them, which was an honor, and got my picture taken with President Clinton.

Dave and I also did some weight training and went for a lot of runs while we were there. Toward the end of our trip Dave asked about my future plans, always looking for improvement. "How are you going to approach your new status in the world of sports? Where are you going in the next few years and how are you going to get there? How do you plan to balance your social and work obligations now that you're in higher demand? What do you need to do to avoid the distractions and continue your training?"

These were tough questions and at first I didn't have the answers.

By the end of the trip, as the sun set over a perfect beach, I told Dave, "I want to be the Lance Armstrong, Michael Johnson, or Muhammad Ali of speed skating."

"Those are things you can achieve, Apolo," Dave said, "which is an amazing and beautiful thing. But you know as well as I do what a commitment it will be and the amount of focus, determination, and effort it will take. You have something that can't be taught—your ability and creativity in your sport—but like you said at the Oscars, it's just the tip of the iceberg. If you want to be the greatest ever, it's not going to always be fun and it definitely won't be easy. But if you make the commitment, mentally and physically, I believe you'll succeed."

Honest, practical Dave. He was right again. I knew that I was not the weak lion getting chased anymore. I was the new young lion protecting my domain yet loving everything around me.

A week after the Dominican Republic trip, I got back on a plane and flew to Montego Bay, Jamaica, for the Met-Rx Superstars, a made-for-TV sports competition held every year to showcase the biggest names in men's sports. I actually missed my original flight and traveled seventeen hours straight to get there. This year the competitors included: Bode Miller (silver medalist in slalom skiing in Salt Lake), Jim Shea (gold medalist in the 2002 skeleton competition), and Jonny Moseley (gold medalist in Nagano for moguls freestyle skiing) competing against NFL players like New York Jets running back Curtis Martin, San Francisco 49ers quarterback Jeff Garcia, Washington Redskins linebacker LaVar Arrington, New England Patriots wide receiver Troy Brown, and "Sugar" Shane Mosley, former WBC welterweight champion.

The competition consisted of individual events—swimming, kayaking, basketball shoot-out, weight lifting, half-mile run, cycling, rock climbing, hundred-yard dash, obstacle course, and Sea-Doo racing. Each athlete had to compete in seven of the ten events and points were awarded for places in every competition.

First up was the basketball shoot-out. There I was, well under six feet tall, with enormous football players talking smack and towering over me. Most of them played basketball before they became football stars. I did horribly. I think I made five points. The next competition was a bike ride. I won, using my anger from my earlier performance to push incredibly hard. During the following event, a half-mile run, I came in third, behind two skiers who were incredibly fast. I skipped the rock climbing competition, because someone told me the wall was overhanging and my strength is all in my lower legs so I thought I didn't have a chance.

The next day we had a fifty-yard swim race. I hadn't been in a pool for years, but I won anyway—I still had some skills. Best by far, was the jet ski competition. The water was so choppy that I couldn't go as fast as I wanted to, because I was one of the smaller guys (compared to the football players) and the waves knocked me off the Jet Ski. Still, I did well and it was exhilarating.

I ended up skipping the weight lifting competition since it was all presses, and the football players had me beat, hands-down. The final "signature" obstacle course, with walls to climb, tunnels, rows of tires, and big tackling pads crushed me. In the high jump the bar was probably at my neck and the guys in the competition were over six feet tall and practically stepped over it. The football players all laughed while I raced through the course. It was an awesome time because it was light and fun and I had the chance to talk to other athletes.

My schedule ever since the Olympics has been truly insane. It's packed with appearances, work on projects, and ever-present training. When I'm not traveling, packing, or unpacking, I'm trying to train and work on projects for my sponsors. It's fast paced, hectic, and I have to use every minute in order to fulfill my responsibilities. I have a lot more help since the 2002 Olympics—IMG, coaches, trainers, and Dave, to help me continue to build upon a foundation of mental strength. As always, my father handles myriad aspects of my career and I don't know what I'd do without him.

Believe me, I'm not complaining about the hectic schedule or the long flights or the appearances. I feel like I've been given the chance to be an ambassador for short track. A lot of people didn't even know what it was before the 2002 Games. Now there are thousands of fans supporting the sport.

I'm also learning how exciting and valuable travel can be. I used to fly to Asia or the Netherlands a few days before a competition, put my head down to train, compete, and then fly home. I'd see the airport (twice), the hotel, arena, and gym facilities. That's it. I failed to see so many beautiful sites and cities. After the Games I decided that I am still going to get rough in competitions, but I also plan to enjoy the other opportunities. I've traveled to Japan many times for events, but I've never tried to understand my roots or see where my dad grew up. In May 2002 my dad and I are going on a trip to Japan to meet family and old friends. I can't wait. I don't just want to fly into a country and focus on getting used to the time zone, hang out in a hotel room and play video games or mess around with friends. I want to see the world and experience it all.

There's no doubt I'm having a lot of fun right now, but my sights are set on the 2006 Olympics. Long after people stop talking about my Olympic moments, I'll be training day in and day out *not* for a handful of gold medals, but to be the best ever—the best short track skater of all time. Skating is what I want to do for the next four years. I love to compete against the elite of my sport and to work on my technique every single day, *because* it's so hard.

An athlete has to love their sport because though the money and fame is nice, there's no guarantee it will happen. Even when there are offers, I've turned very lucrative ones down because they didn't feel appropriate or right. If you love your sport, the people around you, and your opponents, it will make you better and stronger in life and that's what matters.

It's about the journey, and along the way I want to stay true to myself, be generous, loving, and gentle, and take advantage of every opportunity to the fullest. I'm trying to be smart in my decisions but stay true to my heart. My family and friends support me in my efforts, which makes all the difference.

I plan to live an extraordinary life. . . .